Faerie Godmother

(Mythic Series Book One)

Abbie Zanders

To Sheelah,
May all of
your wishes
come true ♡
Abbie Zanders .

Faerie Godmother

Mythic Series, Book One

First edition. December, 2015.

Written by Abbie Zanders.

ISBN: 1532713398
ISBN-13: 978-1532713392

Acknowledgements

Amazing cover design by very talented and skilled Marisa of Cover Me, Darling (covermedarling.com).

Professional editing by the incomparable M. E. Weglarz of megedits.com, a woman with a true gift for spotting plot holes, character anomalies, black holes, and other potential WTFs. Thank you, Meg, from the bottom of my heart.

And special thanks to my beta readers, who brave the first drafts and make invaluable suggestions. This is a better story because of them.

… and THANK YOU to all of *you* for selecting this book – you didn't have to, but you did. Thanks ☺

Before You Begin

Mythic is a standalone series of paranormal romance with plenty of humor and emotion.

Within the pages, you will encounter vampires, shifters, angels, demons, fae, witches, mages, goddesses… just to name a few. It is only recently that these *Extraordinaries*, as they call themselves, coexist peacefully in the idyllic community of Mythic. Very few know of their existence; understandably, they prefer to keep to themselves. However, you've been granted a special look into the world of these amazing being. But be warned --- once you visit Mythic, you might not want to leave.

Chapter 1: Something's Different

"There he is! Quick, grab his arms and help me drag him into the shade."

Vlane heard the voices, but they were oddly muted and far away, as if someone had left that infernal box squawking in the other room again. He tried to open his eyes, but he couldn't. Nor, it seemed, could he roll over. The previous night's party event must have gone much better than expected if he was in this poor condition. He had no conscious memory of imbibing so heavily. Actually, he had no conscious memory of anything, really.

He felt an odd sensation, a stretching kind of pressure in his arms and legs. Was he on a rack, then? In the earlier days of his conversion, it had been one of his favorites. There was nothing quite like having your extremities pulled tight while an entire village doused you with holy water and tried to drive a stake into your heart, mistakenly believing piercing an already-dormant object would matter. Idiots.

Ah, he did miss the Middle Ages. A simpler time, really. Fewer choices. People weren't as educated. Bloodline determined everything, but even across social barriers, there were some universal truths when it came to the undead. Topping that list: Vampires were immortal, barring beheading and being subsequently burned to ash, of course. Only a phoenix could survive *that*.

Another: Vampires were neither damned nor soulless. Many, in fact, were quite pious. They were simply a highly evolved form of a basic human, possessing greater strength, speed, and superior intelligence.

And, after hundreds of years of existence, even vampires could succumb to the inevitable drain of ennui.

It was the last that had begun to overshadow the benefits of the first two these past hundred years or so. Vlane's life had become so predictable, so monotonous, even this slight variation (uncomfortable as it was) was welcome. A bit of pain always enhanced the mundane, as did anything that caused his quiescent neurons to start firing again. Pain, sex, strong emotions — all things Vlane had not personally experienced in a very long time.

Yes, he realized sadly, even this slight discomfort was welcome. If it had been an option, he might have preferred some rather vigorous sex. Though, after several centuries, even that had become rote and bromidic. Women – especially human women – were predictable, and often too frail to sate his carnal hungers adequately. He could follow Kristoff's example and simply indulge in multiple women at one time, thus dividing his focus and subsequently making it easier for a human woman to tolerate, but that wasn't really his style.

At heart, Vlane was an old-fashioned, one-woman-at-a-time kind of guy. In his romanticized ideal, it would be the same woman, over and over again, but alas, he had yet to encounter a single female he wanted to revisit once, let alone repeatedly. They were all the same — barring slight variations in physical appearance, of course. Not one had stood out, or called to him on a level deeper than his cock.

Which was rather disappointing after centuries and centuries of looking for the right one.

"Watch his head. Lift it. No, higher."

A sharp stab of pain at the back of his head preceded a muttered curse (was that Latin?) and a sudden tug upward.

"Oh, sorry about that, Vlane."

The jarring sensation he now felt across his buttocks was even less welcome than the stretching of his limbs. Was he being spanked? Vlane had enjoyed a good caning a time or two, but again, that was more Kristoff's area of expertise. Of course, there was a heady rush to be found in a lush feminine behind blushing from a healthy caress. But this…this wasn't nearly as enjoyable.

Then, just as suddenly, it stopped. The air felt

cooler than it had been only a few minutes ago. The warm, almost-burning sensation across his face and neck faded quickly as the pulling and jarring ceased, leaving his rather bumped and bruised body gloriously still.

"Maybe he needs blood. Open your wrist, Kristoff."

The voice of his long-time friend and sire, Armand, was both comforting and familiar. Something pushed against Vlane's mouth an instant before a cool, metallic liquid began dripping down his throat. At first, it pleased him, and he latched onto the source greedily. But then he was gagging on it, finding the taste wholly foul and unpalatable.

"What the…?" That was definitely Kristoff, the youngest among them at a mere seventy-five. He caught himself before spewing the vulgar modern colloquialisms eschewed by older, more refined vamps. Vlane, eyes still closed, pushed blindly at Kristoff's arm.

"What just happened?" inquired Armand, his angelic voice soft but decidedly clear. Vlane was vaguely aware of Armand leaning over his prone figure, using one of his coveted, centuries-old silk handkerchiefs to wipe at the blood now painting Vlane's face.

"He pushed me away." Kristoff rocked back on his knees, the voice tinged with disbelief and a touch of panic.

Armand, with the practiced calm of the gentle

monk he was, slipped an arm beneath Vlane's shoulders and lifted him to a slightly better angle. "He is delirious. Try again."

Again, something pushed against Vlane's lips. "Drink!" demanded a gruff male voice. Definitely Kristoff. Vlane didn't care at all for his progeny's tone.

He pushed it away again, more forcefully this time. As a five-hundred-year-old vampire, the strength of his shove should have sent the other male flying far away from him, but Kristoff barely moved. He didn't even seem to notice.

"He doesn't want it!"

"*Dios!* Move over, Kristoff. Let me see."

Vlane heard the two males shifting around him. His senses were returning little by little. If he could only see…

His wish was granted when one of his eyelids was lifted and he found himself staring into the face of his housemate. Armand's unnaturally black eyes opened wide as he peered down, though they appeared slightly out of focus, as if Vlane was viewing them through muted filters. His vision was not nearly as crisp and clear as it should have been, and the colors – those few he could discern - were noticeably less vivid.

In fact, none of his senses seemed to be working properly.

"*Dulcis et pia Christus*," Armand breathed in his native Latin, sitting back on his heels as he made the sign of the cross. "Sweet and merciful Christ," he repeated, in English.

"What? What is it?"

Armand turned to Kristoff, shock evident on his beatific face. "He is *human...*"

* * *

Ana always knew she was different. Some of her earliest memories were of sitting alone along the banks of the muddy rivers, perched or straddled along the high limbs of a tree, or, more recently, in the darkened living space behind the Mythic Sanctuary, a specialized facility catering to those creatures of an animalistic nature, particularly shifters. It wasn't that she didn't like people; she did. But over the years, she had learned that even the best intentioned among them could be seduced all too easily by the temptation she offered.

She was used to it, but it still hurt.

It often started so innocently, with well-meaning, sincere desires to do good — easing someone's pain, bringing a bit of joy and hope to those who needed it most, making the world a better place. The trouble was, nothing ever came without a price. Even the most innocuous, seemingly trivial things had the potential to snowball into much bigger issues, often with unintended, far-reaching effects.

Most things, she had come to realize, even bad

things, happened for a reason.

Ana was an inherently gentle soul. She did not want to hurt anyone, and never had, as far as she knew. On the contrary, her particular gift was exactly the opposite. Wherever she went, good fortune and prosperity followed.

Because Ana had the ability to grant wishes.

Oh, not any wish. There were some rules, limits imposed by whatever power had granted her the unusual ability in the first place. But there was very little she couldn't do. And over the years, her mysterious power had only grown. The issue was never whether she *could* alter a situation, but if she *should*.

Then again, sometimes the matter was completely out of her hands.

Ana brought the pads of her fingers to her neck. It was still tender where the dark, handsome stranger punctured her jugular. She'd only been bitten once before, when Bobby Houlihan had come into the diner where she worked with his much younger niece and a couple of girls from her dance class. Good looking, with wavy, blond hair and a shy smile, Bobby had asked her out to the movies when she came to take his order.

Apparently, Casey Martin, younger sibling of Shelly Martin, who everyone knew had a rather unhealthy obsession with Bobby, didn't think that was such a good idea and expressed her opinion by biting Ana's forearm (the Martins weren't the most stable-minded family in the small town, which might explain why Bobby never quite got around to asking Shelly out).

Casey hadn't collapsed on the ground after biting her like the dark, handsome stranger had. But at least Ana didn't go into seizures this time. Clearly, the vampire – *if* that's what he was – had not bitten her with the same malicious intent young Casey had. The sensations Ana had experienced at the dark stranger's hands had been much, *much* different.

Under normal circumstances, Ana had complete control over her gift. She could regulate what, if any, wish would be granted and the extent of it. If someone wished for money, for example, she could gift them with five dollars or five million. But when someone took Ana's blood, *they* became the ones in control of the wish. Their deepest, most heartfelt desires in those crucial moments, whatever they were, came to be.

Casey Martin had wished for Ana to go into a humiliating, full-fledged fit in front of Bobby. What had the dark, handsome vampire wished for?

Whatever it was, it would only be temporary, lasting a few minutes to perhaps several hours, depending on the amount of blood he had ingested and how quickly he metabolized it. In Casey's case, she only got a little taste. Ana's seizures had stopped after several minutes (and before the paramedics arrived, thank goodness), but the vampire had taken several deep pulls before he was overcome. His wish would last longer.

Ana hoped it had been a good one.

Chapter 2: Yep, Definitely Different

It took a good hour for Vlane to regain the use of all of his faculties. He was vaguely aware of his two companions carrying him back to their manor house and settling him onto the oversized sofa in one of the private living areas. Several more times they tried to feed him blood, but each time the result was the same. The coppery taste was vile upon his tongue and made him want to retch. What he really wanted was a big plate of bacon and eggs. Toast. Home fries smothered in ketchup. And orange juice! Dear God, how long had it been since he'd actually had *fruit*?

"It is simply not possible," Armand muttered over and over again. And each time, he would look deeply into Vlane's eyes to confirm what he had already seen a dozen times: Vlane's eyes were a startling, vivid green rather than the typical black eyes of a male vamp, better suited for seeing at night. His skin was warm to the touch, as if his body had absorbed and retained the sunlight in that brief period between the dawn rising and the time they found him (contrary to popular belief, vampires did not burn up in sunlight, but it was uncomfortable). And *his heart was beating.*

"Then you explain it."

Armand looked stunned. Kristoff looked…incensed. As seamlessly as he had stepped into vampiric life, Kristoff had clung to the passion of human emotions longer than most. They, too, faded a bit more every year, but he was still young enough to remember.

"The work of a witch, perhaps?" Kristoff's lip curled up as he said the word. Even among the elitist Otherworldlies (they preferred the term "Extraordinaries", since they did, in fact, share the same world) who made the town of Mythic their home, he had little tolerance for witches. Probably because one of them left him with a rather nasty case of boils when he told her, point-blank, he would not be calling her again as he shoved her out the door after a particularly lusty night.

"I have never heard of a witch with this kind of power," Armand mused. Most Wiccans, in fact, were inherently peace-loving naturalists, using their spells and powers for the greater good (scorned females notwithstanding).

"Have you heard of *anything* with this kind of power?"

Armand shook his head slowly for several long moments as he considered the possibilities, running through the mental checklist he'd no doubt made in his mind (Armand was, by nature, very organized).

From his prone position on the sofa, Vlane could see Kristoff and Armand, both remarkably similar as they paced the room in puzzlement, offering their thoughts. A thousand years separated them in age, but in terms of appearance, they might have been brothers.

"Were?"

"No. They are extremely strong and tend to be rather hairy. Advantageous to have by your side in a brawl or to raze a settlement, but otherwise, not very useful."

"Angel?"

"Perhaps. They are at the top of the magical food chain, but rarely get involved with anyone on earth directly, and they certainly do not bestow or take human life without the express consent of the Supreme Being."

An impressive miscellany of magical Extraordinaries (Exies, for short) resided in Mythic and the surrounding area. The location was akin to magnetic north for the supernatural, though at least one-quarter of the population was fully human. It was a symbiotic relationship of sorts between the myriad of species and races, but for the most part, it worked.

None of them considered the possibility that humans were behind Vlane's unprecedented return to mortality. They had neither the skills nor the knowledge to accomplish such a feat.

"Demon?"

"Probably not. Vlane still has his soul, and no self-respecting demon would go to such effort without taking that."

"Hags, mermaids, leprechauns?" Kristoff speculated.

"No, no, and no." Armand neatly and categorically dismissed each inhuman race as quickly as they arose.

"No," he sighed. "The only type of being I have heard of with that kind of power over life and death are the ancient Fae, the original race, the *Tuatha de Denaan*, the ones who faded away long ago…"

He shook his head faster, dismissing that possibility as well. The Fae had been gone forever, or as close to forever as any of them could conceive. Armand had been around for more than a thousand years and he had *never* seen a vampire turned back into a human. Besides, if there *had* been anyone still around with even a drop of the ancient Faerie bloodline, they would have been captured and exploited a long, long time ago. Fae blood was the ultimate treasure, more valuable than anything else on this entire plane of existence. It was pure, potent magic in ingestible, liquid form.

A sudden gurgle arose from the area of Vlane's midsection, accompanied by a slight, cramping ache. It had been so long, it took him a minute to recognize it for what it was. "I believe I am hungry," he said with equal parts awe and bemusement.

Both males stilled and turned their black gazes his way, looking as incredulous as he felt. Once again, Vlane's stomach rumbled beneath his splayed hand, even louder than the last time.

Vlane rose, using the arm of the sofa to steady himself. Once his sense of equilibrium returned sufficiently, he moved toward the door with hesitant, almost stilted steps. Lifting his legs – which seemed to have become heavier – and placing them just so to remain upright and moving required some effort. When he arrived at the threshold, he tripped.

Kristoff gasped audibly, and Vlane couldn't blame him. Vampires didn't trip.

He turned, a look of surprise on his face, and smiled. "Did you see that?"

Both vamps nodded, completely at a loss to explain it.

They followed Vlane into the kitchen area, watching in stunned silence as he began to root through various cupboards in search of something to assuage the unfamiliar gnawing pain in his belly. Vamps, as a rule, did not ingest anything besides blood, but they usually kept something on hand for their voluntary mortal "guests". There was a decent variety of foods — salty, sweet, tart, and so forth — to satisfy every possible craving. While vampires could not eat the food themselves, they could get a taste of what they desired in the blood of one who could.

"I have often wondered…" Vlane murmured as he pulled various jars and boxes and placed them on the counter. Armand and Kristoff watched in stupefied awe as Vlane crafted himself a sandwich, slathering half an inch of peanut butter on one slice of bread and an equal amount of strawberry jam on the other. Kristoff swallowed hard when he saw Vlane take a bite of the sandwich and chew.

"Oh. My. God," Vlane said, his words muffled by the food in his mouth, but the look on his face was plain enough to see. Pure bliss suffused his features; his eyes rolled back in his head momentarily as his lids closed. He chewed several times, then grabbed a jug of whole milk to wash the sandwich down.

"What is it like?" Kristoff asked, his voice barely above a whisper, all traces of his former arrogance gone as he looked on longingly.

Green eyes sparkled back at him. "Nirvana," Vlane mumbled through the mouthful before stuffing the rest of the PB&J into his mouth and immediately searching for something else to eat.

* * *

Ana was exhausted, but her charges would not be denied the opportunity to sniff, lick, nuzzle, and rub against her upon her return. It was their way of ensuring she was still Ana, and that everything was right in their world.

And it was their world...well, mostly. The remote property, with its state of the art veterinary facilities, had been constructed with animals in mind, not humans. Built by the dominant local pack of Werewolves to care for the special needs of shifters, the massive structure was designed for the pawed, clawed, and hooved, both magical and non-magical alike. At its heart, it was a medical facility, but it also served as a boarding house and sanctuary as well.

As the current live-in caretaker and practicing veterinarian while the pack healer was away, Ana had modest living quarters: a small, cozy bedroom, functional kitchen, full bathroom, and "living" area. The small suite ensured someone was available at all hours of the day or night, which was a definite plus when dealing with the shifters, who tended to sustain more injuries than most other species during "off" hours.

Ana loved them all, and was grateful the Were pack trusted her enough to care for them. She felt more comfortable around them than pure-blooded humans. Here she could be herself (mostly). Those who possessed an animal nature were more likely to live by their instincts and basic needs than getting caught up in so many of the worthless, petty things regular people did.

And, like many of the strays who made this their home, Ana had nowhere else to go.

After checking on them and ensuring they were

all doing well, she took a quick, hot shower, donned a well-worn, oversized nightshirt, and climbed into her big, comfortable bed. She still had a couple of hours before her first scheduled appointment of the morning.

It had been a long night. After fleeing the Masterson Estate, Ana had taken cover in the woods outside of town, half expecting someone to come after her. Leading any danger back to the Sanctuary was the last thing she wanted to do. They had been so kind to her, and had taken her in when she needed a job and a place to stay. It wouldn't do to repay such kindness by bringing vampires to their doorstep.

Only after several hours had passed and no one came looking for her, had she begun the long trek back to her temporary home, keeping to the woods and off the roads, just in case.

Ana sighed and closed her eyes. For now, at least, they were safe.

Chapter 3: Whew, That Was a Close One

By the end of the day, Vlane's healthy complexion started paling again. The vivid green of his eyes darkened, and with each passing hour, his heart beat increasingly slower until it stopped altogether. The warmth of his flesh had faded, and he was once again cool to the touch.

"Whatever it was, it was temporary." Armand looked at Vlane thoughtfully, his index finger rubbing absently at his chin. For all intents and purposes, he looked as unaffected as ever, but through their blood bond, Vlane felt his relief.

Armand and Kristoff had watched over Vlane like mother hens all day, fearing the phenomenon may have been an attempt to make him weak and vulnerable. As a master vampire with his age, skill, and strength, Vlane was undefeatable any other way. If someone had discovered a way to make vampires frangible — even temporarily — they were all in grave danger.

Vlane lounged on the sofa, wearing the weariness of a child who'd spent the entire day at

Disney World. During the last sixteen or so hours, he'd indulged in things unavailable to him as a vampire — eating until his stomach could not possibly hold another bite, relishing the textures and tastes he had not experienced in hundreds of years. He had basked in the sunshine, enjoying the way it felt upon his bare skin, warming him rather than burning. Reveled in the feel of his heart nearly bursting through his chest after running aggressive sprints. Derived pleasure from the strain upon muscles while performing even the simplest of tasks.

He savored every moment, having known no such sensations in a very, very long time.

Now that he was reverting back to his vampiric nature, he could not honestly say he was disappointed. Yes, he had enjoyed the day immensely, but he had forgotten how *hard* it was to be human. The inferior senses. The lack of strength and stamina. The inability to connect with others with a whisper of thought. Such things were foreign to him now. After all, he had only been a human for a mere three decades or so. He had been a vampire for more than five centuries.

And in truth, the blanket of vulnerability had left him feeling rather helpless. Had he not had his loyal brethren watching over him, it might have been far more distressing.

One day spent as a human had been more than enough. Still, he wouldn't have given up this day for anything. Last night, it had been his most heartfelt wish to know what it was like to be human again, if only for a little while...

"What can you tell us?" Armand prodded.

Vlane regarded him thoughtfully. His eyes retained some green around the edges, but the familiar obsidian now filled the center and was expanding slowly outward. The glow of the summer sun clung to his normally pale complexion; it would probably take several days to fade completely.

"Not much, I'm afraid," he admitted, rubbing at the day's growth around his jaw. It felt strange; he hadn't had facial hair in hundreds of years. If he shaved it now, it probably wouldn't grow back unless he willed it to do so. Like everything else, it would remain static, frozen in time — which is why he had been waxing poetic about the continuously changing nature of humans in the first place.

"Surely something out of the ordinary must have happened," Kristoff said, sipping from a wine glass holding a dark ruby liquid. It wasn't wine, but the particular vintage of a middle-aged woman who was an untreated diabetic. Kristoff had a bit of a sweet tooth.

"My mind is a blank," Vlane said on an exhale as he shook his head. He had been attempting to recall the events of the previous evening, but with little success, especially since he'd been so distracted. His last clear memory was of being upstairs in his private office, watching over the annual event via the security cameras with a distant eye.

At one time, Vlane had been a more congenial host and taken part in the festivities, but he had become increasingly reclusive over the years. Immortality and the restlessness of his stagnant existence weighed heavily on him as of late and he was in no mood to surround himself with living, breathing examples of people or beings who changed every day in some small way or another. Not when he didn't, couldn't, and never would again.

He shook his head swiftly, as if that might shake some snippets of elusive recollection back into place. "I was in my office, working on the accounts and occasionally catching a glimpse of the gala. Then…nothing until you two were dragging me inside this morning."

"I think it's safe to say no one forcibly removed you from your office," Kristoff suggested. "So that means something — or someone — obviously got your attention and drew you out. Perhaps the security video will tell us something."

"An excellent idea," agreed Armand.

* * *

"So?" Dani asked excitedly as she bounced into the Sanctuary the following day. "How was it?"

At sixteen, Dani was naturally ebullient. Her

hair, a beautiful shade of amber striated with gold and gathered into a ponytail, bounced right along with the rest of her. Her golden brown eyes were filled with anticipation, her youthful skin radiant with expectation.

Ana barely glanced up from the instruments she was sterilizing. "It was okay."

Dani shot her a stunned look. "Okay? *Okay?!* You were at the masquerade after party at Vlane Masterson's! God, Ana. You are *so* lucky. Do you know what I would give to go to something like that?"

Ana bit back a smile. Yes, she had a pretty good idea. It was all Dani had been able to talk about for the last two months. Apparently, getting an invitation to the event was a big deal — to everyone but Ana. She tried to stay under the radar as often as she possibly could, and going to the year's most celebrated and exclusive local event was not the way to do it. However, with much effort, Dani had convinced her that *not* accepting the invitation would draw more attention than attending and keeping a low profile.

"It was just an after party. No big deal, Dani."

"No big deal. No big deal, she says," Dani lamented, lifting both hands and eyes to the sky as if asking for divine patience. "Did you actually see him? Vlane Masterson, I mean?"

Oh yes, Ana thought. She had seen him. Heard his hypnotic voice, smooth and rich as a double-chocolate milkshake. Breathed in the dark, decadent scent of him, causing desire to unfurl in her belly like a spring bloom on an accelerated time lapse. Felt his cool, moist breath and the hard steel of his body pressed against hers as his fangs pierced the delicate skin of her neck, filling her with the most wonderful sensations…

"Ana? Did you?"

Ana couldn't lie. Like her "gift", she didn't understand it, but there it was — blatant untruths simply could not pass over her lips. She had become quite adept at redirection, however. "Did I what?"

"See. Vlane. Masterson." Dani pronounced each word with particular emphasis. "I heard he is drop-dead gorgeous."

Well, he *was* dead…or undead. Ana wasn't quite sure which was politically correct. But gorgeous seemed inadequate. Vlane Masterson was, quite possibly, the most stunning example of masculine beauty Ana had ever seen. And he was a *vampire*.

"It was a costume party, remember? With masks." For most people, anyway — not *him*, but definitely Ana. Thank God for that. In her faerie princess costume, with the tightly fitted bodice and full, flowing skirt, she'd gone as the Queen of the Fae. It had been Dani's idea, saying Ana's petite, delicate features made her a perfect faerie. The girl really did have a flair for the dramatic. On the plus side, no one recognized her as the antisocial animal doc, though many had tried in vain to guess her identity.

Dani bit her lip, puzzling over that little tidbit. "Yeah, I guess. Did anyone recognize you?"

"*I* didn't recognize me."

Dani giggled. "Yeah, that was kind of the point." Then, sobering a little, Dani looked at her thoughtfully. "You are so pretty, Ana. Why don't you wear any makeup? Or do your hair? Or wear something other than shapeless scrubs and oversized men's clothing?"

"Animals don't care about that kind of thing and neither do I." Hair, makeup, fashionable clothes — those were all things people did to feel better about themselves and garner attention. Ana was quite happy with who she was, and preferred living quietly in the shadows.

"Oh, I don't know about that." Dani countered. "Several of the males were practically pissing on each other over you after the pack meeting last week. Matt threatened to hose them all down if they didn't rein it in."

That made Ana pause. "What?"

Dani smirked. "Yeah. They think you're hot, even for a human. If you were a Were, you'd probably be expecting your first litter by now."

"Well, I'm not," Ana said firmly, hoping it didn't sound too harsh. Dani was pretty much the only female friend she'd made in Mythic. Offending her was not her intention, but the last thing she needed was to become involved with a *werewolf.*

It wasn't that she was prejudiced. The Mythic pack had been very kind and generous, giving her a place to stay in return for medical care until their regular pack healer returned from a personal leave. But until Dani ended up on the operating table nearly a year earlier, Ana hadn't even known they existed. She was still getting used to the idea.

And now she had vampires to factor into the equation. It made her wonder what else was out there, lurking just beyond the blinders of her naiveté. How incredibly close-minded had it been of her to assume she was the only one who was different?

"You can't help what you are, Ana. No amount of denial will change that."

Yeah, no kidding, thought Ana. The question was — what was she?

Chapter 4: Looking for Answers

The three vamps, close friends despite the great disparity in their ages, crowded around the monitors in Vlane's private office.

"There! Look. Who is that?" Armand pointed at the screen directed toward the entranceway. A small female dressed in flowing white silk and jewels stepped into the foyer, looking around as though lost. Her head swiveled this way and that as she clutched her tiny bag and shifted her weight nervously from side to side. The creature nearly jumped a foot when Zarek, the vampire guard watching the door, suddenly appeared in full Gypsy regalia and requested her invitation.

Vlane went still as he felt something fire to life deep within his chest.

"Christ. How did I miss *that*?" Kristoff murmured.

"I do not know," Armand mused. "But I cannot recall her, either."

Three pairs of predatory eyes fixed upon the display as they switched from one camera to another to follow her progress. They watched intently as the delicate figure made her way further into the ballroom, drawing attention and receiving curious, polite nods of greeting by male and female guests alike. While her movements were inherently graceful, they also appeared to be hesitant and uncertain. She gravitated toward the outer edges of the ballroom, seeking the shadows.

It wasn't enough to escape notice, however. Males in particular seemed inexplicably drawn to her. As one after another approached, she shook her head, presumably declining offers of drink and dance.

"It goes on like this for a while," Armand said quietly. He fast-forwarded the images until the tape showed Vlane entering the ballroom, obviously searching for something — or someone. He ignored all attempts to garner his attention, striding purposefully along the edges of the room, his eyes fixed on the open French doors leading out to the balcony.

"Switch to the outside camera on the north side," Vlane said, some vague recollection haunting the edges of his mind, just out of reach.

Armand did so, reaching over to tap the keys. The picture changed, showing the woman at the far end of the balcony. Her back was toward the ballroom, and the camera; her hands rested on the stone wall as she looked out into the perfectly manicured gardens. In the video, Vlane appeared and hesitated briefly before continuing across the polished stone until he stood directly behind her.

The woman gave no indication she was aware of his presence, but that was not unusual. Vampires had the ability to move silently, a necessary skill to avoid frightening their prey.

They remained like that for several long moments. Then, Vlane stepped forward. The woman tensed visibly when he placed his hands on her shoulders, but made no move to flee. Moments later, Vlane swept the gently cascading tendrils of hair to the side, exposing the creamy, peach skin at the delicate curve of her neck. His arms went around her waist and his head lowered slowly, nuzzling as hers drifted to the side.

The silence was heavy as the vampires stared at the screen, transfixed. The woman's body jerked as Vlane struck sure and true, sinking his fangs deep into her vein.

"Christ," whispered Kristoff, tasting his own blood where his fangs had pierced his lip.

In the video, Vlane lifted his head, his face a study in pure, unbridled ecstasy.

And then, he collapsed.

The woman turned, her face still concealed by the mask she wore. Rivulets of dark ruby were clearly visible running the length of her neck and down the expanse of perfect skin, soaking into the shimmering pearlescent white of her bodice. She knelt down beside him and lay her head upon his chest as if listening before turning her attention to his face.

In an exceedingly tender gesture, she pushed the hair away from his brow and placed one hand over his head, the other over his heart. Her lips moved slightly before she released him. With furtive looks toward the ballroom, she backed up enough to pull him out of the pool of light streaming onto the patio. It was obviously a struggle; she was much smaller than the master vampire, but she was tenacious.

With his dark hair and clothing, Vlane melded into the shadows, but the woman's gown reflected enough light to capture her movements. When Vlane was completely out of sight, she leaned down. It was impossible to see exactly what she was doing, but Vlane felt the burn of her kiss upon his lips in tactile remembrance.

And then, she was gone — nothing but a ghostly white blur across the gardens.

"Christ, Vlane," Kristoff murmured. "How could you forget something like that? What did she do to you?"

Vlane couldn't answer him, awash with palpable memories brought forth by the recorded digital images. He remembered the feel of her against him, warm and feminine. The scent of her perfect skin, and the taste of her exquisite blood; he had never had anything like it. It had been like drinking *life* itself, a potent cocktail of sunshine and hope and light, flowing over his tongue, down his throat, suffusing his entire body with a strange, tingling energy.

"Well, I think it is safe to say that whatever it was, it was nothing like we've seen before," Kristoff said, frowning. "Strangely enough, I do not think she meant to harm you in any way. Her reactions seem to suggest she was rather stricken by the turn of events, don't you think?"

Armand did not seem quite as sure. "Such lovely bait," he mused thoughtfully. "A vision of innocence and purity. Irresistible to those like us, who exist in perpetual darkness. I daresay, Kristoff, if Vlane had not spotted her first, you or I may have fallen victim just as easily."

At the thought that one of the others might have discovered her first, an uncharacteristic flare of possessive rage rose up inside Vlane. With considerable effort and centuries of self-discipline, he managed to contain it enough to speak normally. "Where were you, Armand?"

"Snacking," Armand responded absently with a dismissive wave of his hand. As the video feed returned to the ballroom, his figure became visible, re-entering in his Zorro costume with a particularly buxom tavern wench on his arm. As old as he was, he preferred the well-endowed, Rubenesque types — reminiscent of a time when woman were soft and full and didn't try to minimize their natural forms. The woman had the same dazed and pleased look so many of his "snacks" wore afterward.

"What of you?" Vlane asked, turning to

Kristoff.

"Fucking," Kristoff said unapologetically. The few times he'd returned to the ballroom had been brief. It took him only a few minutes to find his next conquests before he was off again, into the nearest alcove or area offering a modicum of privacy. They were necessary concessions for the other guests' comfort more so than his own.

"Neither of you recognize her?" Vlane said, schooling his voice to reveal none of the inner turmoil he felt. Both men shook their heads slightly.

"But I do very much look forward to making her acquaintance," Kristoff said, licking his lips.

Once again, something inherently feral roared up inside Vlane, the intensity nearly making him stagger. He called upon his control, quelling the urge to rip out the throat of anyone who wished to taste her. He had known Armand for most of his life, and Kristoff was like a son to him.

"No one touches her but me," he commanded, his voice dark and deadly. "Find her, but do nothing more. Is that understood?"

Armand and Kristoff exchanged a quick glance.

"As you wish," Armand said smoothly, inclining his head slightly. Kristoff said nothing. With his lips drawn into a thin line, he nodded.

"We have a guest list, do we not?"

"Yes. Zarek and his team ensured everyone in attendance had a proper invitation."

"Then whomever — or *what*ever — that female

is, she was an invited guest. Let us begin there, shall we?"

Chapter 5: Busted

Over the next several days, Ana scanned the local papers for news of anything noteworthy, but found little of interest and nothing particularly worrying. A car accident with minor injuries. A barn fire caused by reckless, partying teens. A few citations for speeding. By the end of the week, she finally began to relax. Obviously, whatever Vlane Masterson's heart's desire had been the night of the ball did not involve mass carnage or apocalyptic destruction. Overall, it had been a very peaceful week in Mythic.

With any luck, he didn't even remember her. Casey Martin hadn't all those years ago. Even as Ana was seizing before her in the grips of some hateful childhood wish, the other girl had no recollection of biting her. And Ana had healed so fast, the bite marks had all but disappeared within a day or two. Unfortunately, it had brought unwanted attention her way and she'd been forced to slip away in the middle of the night before anyone got close enough to learn her secrets.

"Where would you like these?" Matt asked,

breaking Ana away from her morning perusal. She peeked at him over the rim of her massive "I love big mutts and I cannot lie" coffee mug (a gift from Dani) to find him grinning at her with several boxes stacked in his arms.

"Over there would be great," she said, pointing near the desk with the computer. Everything would have to be inventoried before she could restock the shelves. She got up immediately to help him, but staggered backward under the weight of just one box.

"Careful, Ana," he said in his deep, growly voice. "These are heavy."

"Yeah, got that," she said with a rueful smile. He made it look so easy. Then again, Weres were incredibly strong, as she'd discovered. And good-looking. Dani's older brother had the same amber/golden hair and eyes, but he was a good head taller and at least twice as wide. Ana had never seen him shift, but she had seen Dani in her wolf form and she was stunning.

"Thanks for bringing those in," Ana said. "It would have taken me a lot longer."

Samson, the massive Newfie that had just appeared one day, padded over to Matt for an obligatory scratch, while Mr. Whiskers, the black and white mixed-breed feline missing half of one ear, gave him a look of disdain and curled up in the sill of the sunny window.

"Anything for you, Ana," Matt said with a

devastating grin. "You know that."

Heat rushed into her face, but she told herself he meant absolutely nothing by it. Weres, by nature, were as affectionate as they were fierce. He would have been just as kind, just as helpful, to anyone.

"Want some coffee? I just made a fresh pot."

His boyish grin hinted at dimples and showed some very white, very sharp teeth. "I'd love some, thanks." Another thing she'd learned about Weres — they thrived on caffeine.

Matt followed Ana back into her personal quarters.

"So, to what do I owe the honor?" she asked, pulling another mug from one of the hooks beneath the oak cabinets and filling it with her favorite — a rich, hazelnut cream blend.

Matt accepted the cup with a look far too innocent. "What do you mean?"

"I mean, why am I getting a personal visit from the pack Alpha this morning?"

"Can't I just stop by my favorite doc's for a friendly visit?"

"Of course. It's your place, remember?" She paused, taking a sip of her coffee, not believing his presence was as simple as that for one second. And while Matt was a friendly sort, she was sure he had more important things to do than haul boxes or chit-chat over coffee, even if it was darn good coffee.

"Dani asked you to come over, didn't she?"

A slight shrug of those broad shoulders told her

she'd hit that one right on the nose. "She's worried about you. Says you've been acting a little weird since the masquerade ball."

Ana dropped her eyes immediately and turned to add more soy milk to her coffee. The gesture was not lost on Matt, who was used to similar behaviors whenever younger members of the pack were trying to hide something from him. "Weird how?"

"She said you're spooked, nervous, like you're waiting for something to go down. Did something happen at the ball, Ana? Or, more likely, at the after party?"

Ana stirred her coffee without looking up. "Dani has an overactive imagination," she said after several long heartbeats.

"No argument there. But she's also incredibly perceptive. And I can scent your anxiety."

Self-consciously, Ana lowered her head and sniffed discreetly. She had remembered to put on deodorant this morning, hadn't she?

"Is that a nice way of telling me I stink?" she asked.

His full lips quirked. "No. You smell just as exceedingly tasty as you always do, but even more so. A person's natural scent intensifies with their emotions. The more powerfully you feel about something, the more potent your scent — whether it's fear, joy, anger, or…something else."

He emphasized his point by leaning toward her and inhaling deeply. He stilled, closing his eyes as he analyzed the scent. When they opened, they were glittering and...hungry. "And right now, I'd say you're feeling pretty strongly about...something."

Frowning, Ana set her mug down and proceeded to open the windows, wishing the breeze was just a bit more brisk. Yes, she was anxious, half-expecting a pissed-off vampire to show up any minute.

But it was more than that. She'd been unable to get a decent night's rest lately, and the occasional periods of sleep she did manage had been plagued with erotic and frightening dreams. Her natural defenses were wearing thin.

It was impossible to be around someone as innately powerful and masculine as Matt and remain wholly unaffected, especially after last week's bizarre encounter. She'd been feeling sexually frustrated all week, as if the vampire had started something and her body was still looking for completion.

Matt's innate animal magnetism was strong enough to realign her poles on the best of days, but now, in her weakened state, she had to be especially vigilant. She knew it had more to do with nature in general than her specifically; the Alpha would, of course, be the most attractive to the females in his pack, but Ana wasn't a wolf, and should have some measure of immunity to such things.

Matt remained still as she scooted around the tiny kitchen, but his eyes never left her. She could feel them burning into her back, and lower, before settling somewhere around the base of her skull.

"What's going on, Ana?" Was it her imagination, or had his voice deepened?

Being alone with a very large, very strong alpha male in such close proximity was an experience, especially when authority and power radiated from him. Matt and his entire pack had been nothing but wonderful since she'd found Dani broken and bleeding along the highway and tended to her, but she would be a fool not to respect that much power.

They had since become rather protective of her and seemed to like hanging out in the open, airy spaces of the Sanctuary and helping with the animals. Dani said it was because Ana always stocked their favorite snacks and spoiled them rotten, but Ana knew it was as much because of her gift as anything else. Subconsciously, they were drawn to her without knowing why.

Just being around her made them feel good, and she liked having them around. Enjoyed their banter, their teasing. But this week, she had been especially glad for their presence. Every passing moment, she feared Vlane Masterson would show up at her door. Each night, she expected to wake up and find him looming over her like something out of an old Bela Lugosi movie.

Subconsciously, her hand went to the side of her neck. The marks had long since healed, nothing but small discolorations by the time she made it back that night, but the area still tingled whenever she thought about what Vlane had done.

"Something wrong with your neck?" Matt asked, too perceptive for his own good. Clearly, Ana had zoned out again for a few moments. Matt was far closer than she thought he was only a minute before. He stood behind her, his large, looming form completely shadowing her, the heat from his body warming her back.

"I'm fine," she said, and it was technically true. Outside of two small puncture wounds and the loss of a bit of blood, she had suffered no ill effects. Not physical ones, anyway. Erotic dreams involving a certain dark vampire and the awakening of various and sundry female body parts didn't really count as injuries, she rationalized.

She made a move to step away from him, but he stepped forward, positioning his body at an angle so one of his large, muscular legs blocked any further progress. "Let me take a look."

"It's nothing, really," she said rather breathlessly. She hadn't realized exactly how big Matt was until they were only inches apart. Even at a foot and a half away — the accepted standard limit of personal space — he hadn't seemed quite so large. All he had to do was put his arms around her and she felt like she would literally disappear.

But he didn't put his arms around her. More gently than she would have believed possible, Matt pushed the hair away from her neck and tugged her hand away. Ana remained perfectly still, afraid to move, twitch…breathe.

"I won't hurt you," Matt growled softly in that husky voice of his.

"I know," she whispered. But when Matt lowered his face, she began to tremble anyway. Everything about him screamed predator. At that moment, Ana knew exactly what a mouse felt like when a big cat had it pinned.

Matt's face was so close to her skin, she could feel the heat rolling off him in waves, feel the soft caress of his hair against her cheek. He didn't make contact, but he came awfully close, taking a slow, deep inhale.

His eyes closed for a moment and he stepped back, taking another breath. When he opened them again, they were no longer a soft golden brown. They were *glowing*.

"Something you want to tell me, Ana?" he murmured. Now Matt was the one who had gone unnaturally still.

"N-no," she stammered. That was the God's honest truth. She didn't want to tell him. She didn't want to tell anyone. Not about the vampire, or the hot and cold feeling she got from an Alpha being so close.

"Was it given freely?"

Ana's eyes filled with unwanted tears. She hated what a fraidy-cat she was. "Was what given freely?" Her voice was so small, so weak, trembling right along with the rest of her.

"Your blood."

Her big green eyes grew huge as they gazed up at him, shimmering with moisture. "How could you possibly know...?"

"Because he marked you." Ana had never seen Matt truly angry before, but in this moment, he looked downright baneful.

She blinked, several times. Tiny liquid, crystalline prisms adorned her exceptionally long lashes. "Marked me? Marked me how?"

Matt studied her face, as if gaging her sincerity. Finally, his stern expression softened. "You really don't know, do you?"

She shook her head.

He exhaled. "A vampire's venom is unique, like a fingerprint. If one wishes to mark you as his, all he has to do is inject a drop or two. It lets everyone else know he's laid claim, marked you as his territory."

Mild shock gripped her as she sought to make sense of his words. "Kind of like how a dog pees on a tree?"

"Something like that. But it's rare for a vamp to lay claim." He made a noise that sounded like a grunt in the back of his throat. "They're known for their commitment issues."

"Commitment?" she managed weakly.

"Ana, focus. This is very important. *Was your*

blood given freely?" he repeated.

The question wasn't so easily answered. She hadn't offered her blood, nor had she explicitly agreed to let him bite her. He hadn't really asked.

"I-I didn't know he would do that," she said, trying to explain. "I thought he was just going to kiss me…" she spoke slowly, haltingly, feeling kind of stupid now for not realizing what was happening.

"He bit you without your consent?" His eyes were glowing again.

"Maybe he assumed I knew what he was doing." Ana cast her eyes downward. Maybe she didn't know, but her ignorance was no reason to make it seem like a vicious attack. She had actually enjoyed it. The brush of his lips. The feel of his cool breath against her overheated skin. Even the penetration of his fangs had felt good, almost like *sex*. Or, what she imagined sex would feel like. His fangs were long and hard, and in her mind, she had imagined him entering her in more places than her neck.

"I-I didn't try to stop him." *I didn't want to.*

She expected Matt to look at her with disgust, or at the very least, disappointment, but he didn't. "Of course you didn't," he said, barely containing his fury. "Vampires have power. The older they are, the more they have. They get inside your mind."

Had Vlane been inside her mind? She had felt something pressing against her consciousness, but it had been curious, probing — definitely not malicious or controlling. And she was quite sure her innate mental shields had kept him out. Maybe that was why he bit her…

"I'm sorry to have to ask you this, but…did he do anything else?"

"Like what?" Ana asked thickly, no doubt sounding every bit like the innocent she was.

Matt raised his eyebrow and Ana's face flushed a deep, dark red. She was quite glad her mental shields were well developed. There was no way she wanted Matt or anyone else seeing the images that had been a substantial part of her dreams all week.

"Oh, um, no. I barely even realized he'd bitten me before he … uh, fainted."

Matt stilled, tilting his head slightly as if to hear better. "Excuse me?"

"He just…stopped. His eyes rolled back in his head and he dropped to the ground. I-I thought I killed him somehow. But then, I felt a heartbeat and saw his chest rising and falling, so I knew he was just knocked out. I probably should have gone for help, but I panicked. I dragged him out of sight and—"

Matt grew larger right before her very eyes, his features turning angry again. Only this time, it was most definitely directed at her. "Don't lie to me, Ana! Vampires don't breathe and their hearts sure as hell don't beat!"

Ana flinched as if struck, cowering against the counter. "I'm not lying!" she insisted, her voice rising as the tears began to flow. "It's my blood! It does funny things to people…"

Just as quickly as it had come, the anger left his eyes. Matt pulled her gently into his arms, petting her back with oversized hands, as if she were a frightened pup. "Okay, okay. I'm sorry. I didn't mean to scare you. I would never hurt you, you know that. Come over here, sit down, and tell me what is going on."

Maybe it was because Matt was a Were and understood what it was like to be "different". Maybe it was because he made her feel safe; it was impossible to imagine anything bad happening when he was around. Or maybe she had finally reached a critical breaking point and felt the need to unload on whoever was willing to listen.

Whatever the reason, for the first time in her life, Ana found herself voluntarily sharing her story. As she did, she kept thinking how hard it was going to be to have to leave Mythic. She liked it here. But once people knew about her, about what she could do, she would probably have no other choice but to leave. It was a bittersweet moment, but once she started, she could no more stop the flow of words than she could turn back time.

Matt listened carefully, filling his coffee mug and hers several times over the course of her explanation. When Ana finally fell silent, she looked up into his face, not knowing what she would find.

His expression was thoughtful, almost bemused. "So...basically, what you're telling me is...you can grant wishes?"

She inhaled, exhaled, and nodded. "Yes."

"Anything?"

She shrugged. "I won't knowingly harm someone. I try to consider all possible ramifications before I grant a wish. But other than that, yeah, I think so."

"If I wanted a thick, juicy hamburger right now, you could make that happen?"

She nodded.

"Would you?"

Ana sighed. She knew it would come to this — a request of proof — but she couldn't blame him. The whole thing sounded like something out of a children's book. At least he didn't ask her for something ridiculous.

She reached across the counter and lightly took his hand; physical contact was helpful in making the wish happen. She blinked slowly, holding his gaze with her pale green eyes. "You want fries with that?"

Matt felt the gentlest of tugs deep inside him, almost a tickle. Then, a thick, juicy burger appeared before him, complete with thick-cut seasoned fries and a pickle spear.

Matt looked down at the plate in awe. "Jesus. Where did this come from?"

"My fridge," she sighed. "I don't have the

power to create something from nothing, but I can kind of…rearrange things. Move them. Manipulate them. Or, in this case, cook them."

"Jesus," he repeated. Ana grabbed a French fry from his plate and munched on it, waiting for him to fully grasp the implications, and wondering what he would do with that knowledge when he did. Would he tell the others? Would it change the way he looked at her? Would he start asking her to do things for him? For his pack?

She felt the first twinge of sadness, knowing with this knowledge came the beginning of the end of her brief, but truly happy time here.

"Are you some kind of djinn or something? A goddess? A Faerie?"

"I don't know what I am," she admitted.

"But your parents, they must have told you something. Did they have powers like this?"

"I don't know that, either. I never met them." Years and years of being alone, not really knowing anything about where she came from. But she didn't tell him that. He was already looking at her in that overly protective way he had. She didn't need to give him even more of a reason to feel like some kind of charity case.

"Does anyone else know?"

"No. Just you."

He blinked slowly, obviously realizing she had just shared with him something she had not shared with anyone else. "No one?"

She shook her head. "You're the first," she said with a small smile. "I don't advertise it. If people knew…" She let the sentence hang.

"They'd never leave you alone," Matt finished, wrapping his big hand around hers. "I don't know what to say. I'm honored you would place that kind of trust and faith in me."

Ana remained quiet. Perhaps it was selfish of her, but if felt so good to finally share it with someone, even if it could only be for a little while.

The hand-crafted wooden clock ticked with each passing second, sounding louder than it should have in the silence of the small kitchen. Outside, the gentle early morning breeze carried the sound of approaching voices, probably her first patients of the day. Ana took a chance and lifted her gaze to Matt's. What she saw there was unexpected. Determination. Respect. Humility.

"Your secret is safe with me, Ana. I won't let anyone hurt you. Consider yourself under the protection of the pack."

He didn't offer the words lightly. Over the past year, she had learned just how tight Were packs were. Even she knew they accepted no outsiders. She had been lucky enough to befriend them because of what she had done for Dani.

"I'm not a Were."

He shrugged, as if the concern was irrelevant. "You could be." He pinned his golden eyes on hers, a silent offer. As Alpha of the pack, she knew, he could turn her, make her one of them.

Ana opened her mouth to say something, but no words came. "Just think about it, okay?" he said, squeezing her hand. "Until then, consider yourself an honorary member."

She nodded, taking a deep breath, feeling both relieved and scared to death at the same time.

"Mind if I take this with me?" he said, pointing at the burger with a hungry smile. "It smells awesome. Not quite as good as you do, but…"

The teasing twinkle was back in his eye, and Ana couldn't help but smile. "Knock yourself out. I don't even eat meat. I just keep it around for you guys."

Matt's grin grew. "No wonder the adolescents love it here. You spoil them, Ana."

A genuine smile lit her features, reaching her eyes. "They're good kids. And very helpful."

"Don't let them hear you say that. They'll never leave."

Ana laughed, releasing some of the tension. Now she just felt drained. Matt bent down and gave her an affectionate kiss on the cheek at the sound of the outer door opening. "We'll talk more about this later, but be careful, Ana."

"I'm always careful." But sometimes things happened anyway.

He cast her a doubtful look and slipped something into her hand.

"What's this?" she asked, looking at the thin

metallic cylinder on a silver chain.

"A special whistle, pitched at the right frequency for Weres. Keep it with you at all times. You blow that at the first sign of trouble and you'll have the pack at your doorstep in a heartbeat, hear me?"

"Thanks, Matt," she said, looping the whistle over her head and tucking it into her scrub top. She hoped she'd never have to use it, but it did provide a much-needed sense of security.

They emerged together into the waiting room, where Mrs. Peterson was clutching a miserable looking toy poodle dressed in a pink satin jacket. She eyed both of them and smiled broadly.

"Good morning, Dr. Ana, Mr. Gullwolff."

"Good morning, Mrs. Peterson." Matt offered a boyish smile and tipped his head, earning a glowing smile from the older woman.

"I'll send one of the boys over later to move the rest of those boxes for you, Ana."

Both Ana and Mrs. Peterson watched Matt's retreating figure.

"Oh, Dr. Ana!" the older woman twittered. "I think he likes you!"

"He's a good friend, Mrs. Peterson," Ana clarified in an attempt to nip that rumor right in the bud.

"Of course, dear," she said, still grinning from ear to ear. "Whatever you say…"

Chapter 6: Come to My Web...

Every year, the Mythic Masquerade Ball was held at the Mythic Community Center on the eve of the summer solstice. It was one of the few days celebrated by the vast majority of Extraordinaries for very different reasons, and open to the entire town, humans included.

But the after party at Vlane Masterson's palatial estate, which most considered to be the real event, was by invitation only. Who might receive the much sought-after, hand-delivered expensive vellum was a constant source of speculation. No one knew the criteria used to create the list, only that wealth, notoriety, and social status had little to do with it. An invitation one year certainly did not guarantee one the next.

There were, however, a respectable amount of "regulars" (mostly immortals) who came to enjoy Vlane's exceptional and generous offerings. Since Vlane was quite sure he had never come across whomever, or *whatever,* had disrupted his rigidly static existence so spectacularly, he didn't bother with them. That cut down the list considerably, leaving only a sparse dozen or so female newcomers.

By the end of that first week, they had managed to eliminate all but three.

"What of the others?" Vlane asked, feeling an immense sense of relief when the vapid blonde was finally ushered over the threshold (rather reluctantly on her part). It had only taken a moment for him to realize she had been invited as a boon to Kristoff, who had heard the woman was especially skilled in various forms of unusual erotic play, a fact Kristoff later confirmed with a smug smile and a gleam in his eye.

Armand examined the list, though they had long since committed it to memory. They had thought of little else. Living as long as they had and finding something so truly puzzling, quite possibly the only real threat they had faced in centuries, presented an irresistible challenge.

"Marilyn Connors is currently in the hospital, the result of a car accident several days ago. She is in a semi-private room, but her roommate was discharged earlier today, so we should have no difficulty slipping in tonight to speak with her."

Vlane nodded. "Very well."

"Trudy Anderson seems to have vanished," Kristoff said with a frown. "She was last seen with some of Karthik's demons at *Seven Circles*." *Seven Circles* was a BDSM nightclub on the outskirts of Mythic, a popular place for those who had hardcore hungers. "Word is, she seeks to become permanent staff."

Translation: she was willing to sell her soul to the demon lord for the chance of eternal youth. Vlane wondered if she knew Karthik required a minimum of one hundred years indentured service as part of his price for immortality. Vlane sincerely hoped the woman he sought was not Trudy Anderson. Much, if not all, of the potent life energy he'd sensed would be drained from her well before her time was up.

"Karthik is the possessive sort," Vlane mused aloud. "He's not likely to respond if he believes we have more than a passing interest in the girl. Talk to him directly. Assure him that I wish to speak with the woman while she still maintains some of her faculties. I will need no more than a few seconds to know if she is the one we seek."

"And if she is?"

"Then things will become complicated. Let us hope that is not the case."

Kristoff nodded his acknowledgement.

"And the third? What do we know of her?"

"Ana McKinnon. She is a vet," Armand answered.

"Excuse me?"

"A veterinarian," Armand clarified. "An animal doctor."

"I know what a veterinarian is," Vlane snapped impatiently. The entire situation had him on edge. "Why have we not spoken with her yet?"

Armand and Kristoff exchanged an

uncomfortable glance. "She is under the protection of Matthew's pack."

"Is she a Werewolf?"

"Not as far as we know."

Vlane considered this. He sat back in his chair and tented his fingers in front of his face. "It is unlike Matthew to extend his reach beyond his own kind."

Despite the potential danger this strange creature presented, Vlane's interest was piqued. Not only had she managed to temporarily strip him of his vampiric strengths and render him vulnerable, but she had also ensconced herself among a tight-knit community not known for their acceptance of outsiders.

What exactly was her relationship with Matthew and his pack? And more importantly, was the Mythic Alpha privy to her unusual ability? The relatively recent peace accord between the wolves and the vampires was friable at best. If either side had knowledge of how to incapacitate the other, it would upset the delicate balance and throw them back into the open hostilities which had plagued both sides for centuries.

"True. But he credits the woman with saving the life of his youngest sister, Danielle, last autumn," Kristoff supplied. "It was ugly. Some human hunters shot the whelp, but she managed to escape before they could get to her. Most unfortunately for her, she stumbled onto the highway and was hit by a car. Ana McKinnon happened to be driving by, saw the poor creature, and rendered aid. By the time Matthew's brutes located her, the good doctor already had things well in hand."

"What kind of woman picks up a badly injured wolf from the roadside?" Vlane mused softly.

"One with no sense of self-preservation," quipped Armand.

"Indeed," Vlane murmured. The very thought intrigued him. Might that same lack of self-preservation be why the woman found herself in a nest of vampires and Extraordinaries? Or was her purpose here a much darker one?

He knew which he preferred. Their brief encounter had left him wanting to know more; it would be a shame if her timely appearance was meant to be his downfall.

"Let us extend an invitation to Dr. McKinnon, shall we? Under the circumstances, it might be better to hold our little meeting away from Matthew's watchful eye."

* * *

Ana looked at the gold-embossed vellum in her hand as if it might bite her.

*The honor of your presence
is requested
for cocktails and a light repast
at seven-thirty tomorrow evening.
Masterson Estate*

She re-read it at least three times before the man who delivered it cleared his throat quietly, reminding her of his presence. He looked to be around twenty or so, just past boyhood, with dark eyes framed by sinfully dark lashes against pale skin and exquisitely chiseled features, though he was too masculine to truly be considered "pretty".

"I am to await your response," he explained apologetically. His words held the slightest hint of an accent, making her think vaguely of the Mediterranean. Corsica, perhaps? Or maybe Crete.

"My response?"

"Yes, ma'am," he said with a patient smile.

"Oh. Of course. I'm sorry. Please, won't you come in?" Ana felt the color rising in her cheeks, a bit embarrassed. She was not familiar with the proper etiquette for dealing with a formal dinner invitation. No one had ever issued her one before.

"Can I offer you something to drink?" she asked.

She thought she saw a devilish twinkle in his

eye, but it was gone too quickly for her to be sure. There was no mistaking his amusement, however. "Thank you, ma'am, but no."

"Honestly, do you have to call me ma'am? You don't look any older than I do."

"I meant no offense, Doctor."

"Ana, please."

"*Ana*." She felt a slight ripple run down her spine as the man spoke her name softly.

Still wearing her animal print scrubs (mint green with big fluffy white lambs), Ana proceeded to the reception desk and reached for a pen. She thought about it for a moment, then scribbled a few words on what she guessed was the response card. When she was finished, she tucked everything back into the expensive-looking envelope and handed it to him.

She received a genuine smile in response before he bid her a good day.

* * *

When Jason returned to the Masterson Estate, he went directly to Vlane's private office as instructed, and handed him the envelope.

"You saw to this personally?" Vlane asked, forcing himself not to snatch it out of his progeny's hand. Like Kristoff, Vlane had brought Jason into the vampire life at the young man's dying request. Unlike some sires, Vlane felt a personal responsibility to those he'd turned, and ensured that any of his bloodline held a position within his household if they so wished.

"Yes, sire."

"And how do you find her?"

Jason's lips quirked when he recalled the strange garb adorned with fluffy white sheep and the riot of golden hair refusing to remain neatly coiffed in the clip meant to hold it. "She was…interesting." He hesitated, unable to suppress the slight tilt to his lips. "She willingly offered me her name."

"Her *real* name?" Most people had human monikers assigned to them, created by ignorant parents for ridiculous reasons. Those held no power whatsoever. But a being's true name, the one inscribed in the Book of Souls, was priceless. Very few actually knew theirs until they stood before the Scribes of Judgment. The fact that she did — and was quite open about it — was rather confounding.

It was entirely possible she was ignorant of such things; that she had no idea names held great power, especially in the hands of one who could wield and shape it like a man of Jason's caliber. He was a vampire, yes, and had been for nearly two hundred years, but as a human, he had been a practicing sorcerer, apprenticing under one of the greatest mages of Eastern Europe. The fact that she had given her name — her real one based on her reaction when he spoke it — suggested she was every bit as innocent and naïve as she appeared. Either that, or she was laying yet another ingenious trap.

Vlane's eyes narrowed, but Jason said nothing more. Vlane extracted the small notecard and saw the delicate, feminine script:

> Thank you for your thoughtful
> invitation. However, I must
> regretfully decline.

"She declined?" Armand said in disbelief, looking over Vlane's shoulder. Vlane waved at the note card. Armand picked it up and studied it as if he had never seen such a thing before. "She *declined!*"

"So it would appear," Vlane said with the hint of a smile. Now he was more intrigued than ever.

The visit to Marilyn Connors' hospital room was brief, lasting barely more than a minute or two. She was sleeping under sedation when they arrived. Vlane took one look at the form beneath the sterile, white sheets and camel-colored thermal blanket and knew she was not the woman he had tasted. She was much too tall, too broad-boned. Her features, while attractive, held no recognition for him. In the interest of thoroughness, however, he leaned down close to her neck and inhaled deeply. Her scent was mild and unremarkable; nothing like the one he sought at all.

He shook his head. "It is not her."

They left as quietly as they came.

Vlane turned the glass in his hand, his eyes fixed upon the dark red liquid. At one time, this particular human's blood had been one of his favorites, but it no longer held the pleasure it once had. Compared to *her* taste, it was flat. Dull. Lifeless.

Kristoff had yet to speak with Karthik about Trudy Anderson (the demon was being particularly evasive) but it mattered little. Vlane no longer believed her to be his mysterious guest. Perhaps he was wrong, but he did not think the woman he was looking for would have sold herself so cheaply to the likes of a demon, even a powerful demon lord such as Karthik. And if she had, Karthik would be crowing about it to every immortal within a hundred miles.

No. The woman he sought would have plucked a bloodied and battered lethal she-wolf from the side of the road and tried to save it.

She would have the temerity to oh-so-politely decline his personal, exclusive invitation.

Dr. Ana McKinnon was the one he was looking for. He felt it in his very bones.

Chapter 7: Another Offer

"Why was Jason here?" Matt asked, tilting his face ever so slightly and subtly sniffing the air.

Ana's hands clutched the glass of warm, sweetened milk. People had been in and out all day, but she had wiped down the entire waiting area with an organic antiseptic because of a particularly messy emergency not long before. A pleasant hint of lemons still hung in the air.

"How can you possibly distinguish one person's scent after I just cleaned?"

He grinned. "I can't. One of the brutes saw him leaving and told me about it." He leaned toward her and inhaled. "I can, however, smell *you*." His eyes closed and a smile curved his lips. "It's something new, isn't it?"

Yes, it was. Something she had hoped might mask her "natural" scent in case vampires had the same scent-signature-recognition thing the werewolves had going on.

He opened his eyes and shot her a heart-stopping grin. "I like it. Makes me think of tropical beaches and sunsets."

Ana's cheeks flamed red. Wearing comfortable

harem-style sweats and a loose fitting tank (her favorite sleepwear), even she could easily smell the vanilla and coconut body butter. She indulged in the calming scents whenever she was feeling particularly anxious.

"So, what did he want?" Matt asked, pinning her with his intense gaze.

"Who?" A mental image of Matt's finely honed body on display in nothing but swim trunks rose unbidden the moment he mentioned tropical beaches and sunsets. It was difficult to concentrate on anything else. He was the walking personification of hot and sweaty sex, calling to anything with double-X chromosomes. Making matters worse, this past week she'd been a pathetic and highly combustive cocktail of female hormones.

"Jason," Matt repeated, his eyes twinkling. Oh yes, he'd probably guessed the direction her thoughts had taken. Clever wolf.

"Who is Jason?"

"He's one of Masterson's minions. Is he harassing you?"

Ana realized he was talking about the good-looking man who had brought her the invitation. She should have known he was a vamp. Human men weren't that perfect.

"Oh. No, nothing like that. Is that why you came all the way over here?"

"It's not that far," he hedged. "And seeing you

in your jammies is always a nice way to end the
day. What did he want, Ana?"

She blew out a breath, crossing her arms to
hide the way her nipples hardened under Matt's
gaze. Damn him and his Alpha pheromones when
her hormones were preparing to revolt and overrun
her common sense and propriety. The beast in him
could probably scent it, too. "He just delivered an
invitation."

"To what?"

Ana hesitated. "Dinner, I think."

"With Masterson?"

"I assume so, but it didn't say that
specifically."

"And?"

"And I declined. End of story."

Matt shook his head. "Clearly, you have no
concept of the male psyche. Don't you know it's all
about the chase? All you've done is wave a red flag
in front of a blood-sucking bull."

She stared at him, bemused. Matt leaned
forward and pushed a stray, riotous curl away from
her face. She blinked, but the rest of her went
completely still as she held her breath.

"I won't hurt you," he breathed in exasperation.

"I know," she whispered, but she still couldn't
keep herself from trembling a little. While her mind
might understand he was her friend, the more
primitive parts of her brain recognized him for what
he was — a very large, very dangerous, Alpha

predator.

What she didn't know was if her reaction was based on fear or his irrefutable sexuality. Male wolves made no attempt to hide their base sensuality, and Matt had it in spades. She wondered idly if he'd chosen a mate yet. According to Dani, he was looking. A male in his prime was expected to sire, and Matt was definitely in his prime. He oozed virility.

And yet, the sexually charged Alpha wolf was not the one consuming her dreams and a substantial part of her waking moments.

"Do you think Masterson remembers you?" he asked, breaking into thoughts she had no business thinking.

"I don't know what to think," she said, shaking her head to rise above her fear...or whatever that tingly, anxious feeling was. "It was a formal invitation. Maybe he sent it out to a bunch of people."

"Is that what you believe, Ana?" He was closer now, his presence a tangible thing around her.

"No," she answered, her voice reverting to a whisper. When Matt was this close, he literally stole her breath away. "I think he suspects that whatever happened has something to do with me."

"You are frightened."

There was no use denying it. Surely, he could scent her fear. Hopefully it overpowered every other possible fragrance she might inadvertently be producing. "Yes."

"I can protect you, Ana."

Though she appreciated the offer, she shook her head immediately. She had only been in Vlane Masterson's presence for a short time, but she had never felt anything quite so powerful. Even a strapping Alpha like Matt might not be able to fight against him. It was her problem, not his. She liked him too much to put him in danger.

Besides, his pack needed him. She was expendable.

"No, Matt. I couldn't bear it if anything happened to you or your pack because of me."

"I could mark you. Make you one of us."

"You said *he* marked me."

"He did, but only partially."

"What does that mean?"

Matt blew out a breath. "His mark is very faint, which means he probably didn't even mean for it to happen. My guess is it happened accidentally when you whammied him. He doesn't realize what he did, I know that much."

"How could you possibly know that?"

He shifted his weight uncomfortably, and anything that made Matt uncomfortable sent ripples of terror through her. "Because he would know he already has a link to you. Masterson has been around a long time, Ana. He's an expert in mind control and manipulation. If he wanted to, he could simply invoke the link and summon you. You would have no choice but to comply."

The color drained from her face. "You knew this and you didn't tell me?"

"You led me to believe he would have no recollection of what happened, so I didn't want to worry you unnecessarily. But now he's sniffing around you and I'm no longer willing to take that chance."

Ana hugged herself tightly, subconsciously trying to make herself as small and insignificant as possible.

"And what do you propose?"

* * *

Her eyes, as wide as saucers, tugged at something deep in his gut. He watched as her expression changed from one of shock, to anger, to fear. He didn't like seeing fear on her face; it had no business there.

Unlike the females of his kind, Ana did not have natural instincts urging her to fight. Hers had her cowering and trying to make herself as small as possible in the hopes of being viewed as not worth the effort. The little bit of nervousness she normally felt in his presence was flattering, but this was different. His natural instinct to protect rose to the surface.

She had reason to be afraid. Vlane Masterson wouldn't send his best spymaster on an errand without good reason, but he didn't want to worry Ana by telling her that. His acute hearing could pick up the erratic staccato of her heartbeat, and he didn't think it was all due to him (though, he could hope). The fact that he could scent warm, sweetened milk in the mug in front of her indicated she'd been anxious even before he arrived.

Though her normally delicious scent *had* magnified since then.

His golden eyes met hers. "Let me mark you, Ana. My mark will be stronger than his, because I will make it so."

"And…how would you do that, exactly?"

He leaned in closer, wrapping her in blazing heat that silently promised she would never, ever be cold again. He stroked the roughened pads of his big fingers against the tender skin where her neck met her shoulders, making her shiver. "A bite. Here."

A scant few inches of insubstantial space separated his mouth from her skin; not enough to keep the feel of his mint-scented, hot breath from dancing across the surface.

"Would it hurt?"

"Yes," he murmured. He would not lie to her. There was nothing gentle about a wolf's claiming of another; it was viscerally carnal in nature. But he could distract her while he did it. At the height of an orgasm was ideal. Her body would be so consumed with ecstasy, the pain would enhance the experience. "But there are ways to make the pain pleasurable."

He leaned in even closer and inhaled deeply. He could take her, so easily. Ease her fears, make sure she was never afraid of anything ever again. "Christ, you smell good." He brushed his lips against her neck as his hands clamped down firmly on her shoulders.

She trembled beneath him. "Don't move, Ana. I don't want to tear your beautiful skin…" That was a lie. He wanted to ravage her, make his claim so obvious no one, of any race, would ever question it.

"Matt, wait," she gasped. "What is it that *you* want?"

"What?" he murmured against her skin, his tongue peeking out to lick. He moaned at the taste of her. It was even better than her scent. The beast in him roared to claim her.

"What is it your heart desires most?"

"To keep you safe." That was the man talking. The beast's answer was more honest: *To claim you. To mount you and make you my mate.*

"Matt, are you certain? It's important."

So consumed by her scent, by her taste, it was only at the farthest reaches of his consciousness he heard her words at all. "Why?"

"If you take my blood, whatever you most wish for in that moment will come to pass."

His canines lengthened, scraped lightly against her skin. "You can stop me if I go too far." But he hoped she wouldn't. Now that her scent filled his lungs and her taste was in his mouth, he wanted more. A lot more. She was delicious, and he wanted to hear her screaming his name in mindless ecstasy. She was in her heat cycle, he could smell it, he could get pups in her tonight…

"No, I can't. When you take my blood, I have no control over what happens. And after that first drop, neither will you."

Matt stilled, forcing himself to rein in the painful need to claim her. He leaned back slightly and looked into her eyes, so big and green. It was like diving into a tropical sea. She was too small, too fragile to stop him.

He could just take what he wanted and make it up to her later. She wouldn't be sorry. He would be a good mate. There was no one stronger, no one who could protect her better. Not even Vlane Masterson would be arrogant enough to attempt to take an Alpha's mate.

But she hadn't actually agreed, had she? Free will was paramount to his kind. An honorable Were male would only accept a female who had openly and deliberately chosen him. "Do you want this, Ana?"

"No," she whispered, tears falling silently down her cheeks. "Not like this."

Not like this. Not under duress. Not against her will. Several long moments passed while Matt fought against his primal urges. Ana lifted her hand

and began to stroke the back of his head gently while placing the other lightly on his shoulder. It helped to soothe him; to remind him that while he was part beast, she was not. Maybe someday she would be, but she was not ready, and Matt would not make that decision for her unless it became a matter of life and death, no matter how much he wanted to.

He took a deep, shuddering breath. "I'm sorry. I don't think it's safe for me to be around you right now," he said as he stepped backward, putting more distance between them. His voice was barely human, rougher than usual. "I'll send some of the others over to keep watch."

She nodded slightly, clearly afraid to move or speak or do anything that might threaten the tenuous thread of control to which he clung.

Matt walked through the door, shifted immediately into his wolf form, and ran away from her tempting scent, howling out orders as he went.

Chapter 8: Bond, Vampire Bond

Vlane stood at approximately the same place she had that night, according to the security cameras. He placed his hands, palms down, in the same way she had, feeling the cool stone beneath his fingertips. Looking out over the fine gardens, he took in the neatly trimmed hedges and bushes and the abundance of annuals and perennials in full summer splendor, glowing faintly in the light of the moon.

What had she seen when she stood here? Did she see the complex designs and patterns he had created himself, based on some of the most exquisite gardens in history? Did she recognize any of the rare and exotic species it had taken him years to procure and collect? Or did she simply see beauty?

The events of that night were coming back to him, little by little. At least, he thought they were. Perhaps it was just that he had privately reviewed the security footage so many times over the past few days his mind had begun to assimilate those images as actual memories. He wasn't even sure it mattered anymore.

He closed his eyes, and there she was, just like the video had captured her. In a shimmering white gown with a full skirt that kissed the tops of her toes, and a snug, laced bodice that accentuated the perfect hourglass of her form and plumped up her ample breasts to create just the slightest suggestion of what lay beneath. Her sleeves extended just past her shoulders, baring toned, feminine arms. He had touched her skin there. It had been warm and soft, like heated silk, begging to be stroked and kissed…

Her hair had been pinned up rather haphazardly, or so he thought. The result was a series of tiny cascades around her delicate face, while bigger curls of spun gold verged on escape at any moment. A few loose waves managed to tumble over the curve of her neck, along her shoulders. It was those he had pushed aside to bare the graceful curve of her neck.

The shimmering gold mask she wore concealed a good deal of her face. But he *had* seen her eyes. They were an unusual shade of green, unlike any he'd seen before. Cut and faceted, but clear, as if crafted by a master jeweler.

And her lips…he could compose sonnets about her lips. Delicate yet full, the exact shade of a perfect pink Asiatic lily, arguably one of his favorite blooms. He now wished he had tasted those lips, certain they would have been soft, so very soft, and tasted so very good…

Vlane slammed his hand upon the stone in a

rare show of frustration. He wanted her. Here. Now. So he could glean once and for all whether she had been deliberately sent to wreak havoc upon him or it had been a trick of the fickle Fates. He did not want to discover that her appearance had been staged or that she was the possible harbinger of his downfall.

No. What he wanted would be infinitely more devastating.

For the first time in his life, Vlane wanted more than a woman's blood or her body.

From this woman, he wanted *everything*.

He looked up at the moon again, waxing toward its apex. He knew where she was. Scarcely half an hour's drive away; he could traverse the distance in a matter of minutes with his preternatural speed. However, it would be inadvisable for him to visit her now. The Sanctuary was located on the outer fringes of Matthew's territory. The pack's aggressive natures would be peaking soon with the full moon, and all indications pointed to the Weres being quite protective of her.

Yet, he didn't want to wait. Normally a man with infinite patience, it now seemed he had none whatsoever.

If only she would come to him…

"Ana," he whispered into the breeze, closing his eyes again. "Why do you play this game with me?"

* * *

Ana's eyes popped open. She had been dreaming of the vampire again, but something had woken her. She sat up and looked around her room. Moonlight poured in through the windows where a soft breeze carried cool air and the scent of wild honeysuckle.

Satisfied she was alone, Ana fell back to her pillow with a moan. Like every other time she had dreamed of him, her body was uncomfortably hot and achy. Of course, what had happened earlier with Matt hadn't helped. She might not be ready to be his mate, but the man did have some serious sexual mojo going on.

"You are cruel to torment me like this."

Ana gasped. She heard a man's voice. *Vlane Masterson's voice! In her head!* She stilled immediately, listening in the silence to hear it again.

"You cannot hide among the wolves forever, little Ana. I know you are the one I seek..."

For the second time that night, Ana found herself trembling. Her heart pounded against her chest so forcefully, she was sure he must hear it. Had Vlane finally remembered he had marked her? Was he truly talking to her, or was he just broadcasting his thoughts without realizing she could hear him?

He didn't seem to expect her to answer, and there was no indication he had heard her thoughts or sensed her panic. Perhaps the communication only traveled one way. Matt hadn't been very specific about how that marking connection thing worked. He just said if Vlane knew he had created a bond between them, he would be able to summon her at will…

The thought sent a shiver down her spine. Vlane hadn't summoned her, even though he clearly wanted to, based on those last few statements. So maybe he really didn't remember…

The phone beside her bed rang, startling her. Ana debated whether she should answer it. What if it was Vlane?

Then again, it might be a true emergency. This *was* an animal hospital, and one of the reasons she lived here was so that she could provide twenty-four hour care if necessary. It wouldn't be the first time someone had gotten themselves hurt in the middle of the night.

The answering machine was located at the front desk. She could just let that pick up and then check it. Feeling somewhat ashamed for allowing her fear to influence her, Ana got out of bed and padded toward the office area. The machine kicked on after the fourth ring, but when it came time to leave a message, there were only a few seconds of silence and then the snick of an ended connection.

Even as she stood there, leaning uncertainly against the wall, the phone rang again. And again, the unknown caller left no message.

Who was calling at such an odd hour and hanging up? If there really was an emergency, wouldn't someone leave a frantic message or something?

As she pondered that, a heavy knock pounded at the door. Ana cowered in the shadows of a large, decorative palm, out of sight of whoever it might be.

"Ana! It's Derrick! Open the door!"

Ana breathed a sigh a relief. Derrick was one of the teen brutes who belonged to Matt's pack.

"Derrick?" she said, opening the door. "What are you doing here? Is someone hurt?" She quickly looked him up and down, searching for injury, but he seemed just as solid and healthy as ever.

The teen, who towered over her and outweighed her by a good eighty or ninety pounds, stepped into the waiting room area and closed the door. "Yeah, she's here," he said into a smartphone. "Hang on." He held the phone out to Ana. "It's Matt. He wants to talk to you."

She snatched the phone out of his hand. "Matt? What's wrong? Are you alright?"

On the other end of the phone, Matt exhaled a huge sigh of relief. "I'm fine, Ana. Why aren't you answering the phone?"

Ana felt the anxiety leave her in a rush, replaced by mild irritation. "I'm screening. Why are you calling me in the middle of the night?"

"I frightened you again, didn't I?"

"You didn't leave a message. I didn't know what to think."

There was a pause. "I can't sleep. I had a feeling you couldn't either. I wanted to call and apologize for my behavior earlier. That's not the sort of message you leave on a machine. I'm sorry. I never should have lost control like that."

Ana glanced at the teen, wondering if his hearing was acute enough to pick up what Matt was saying. "Derrick," she said, wanting to keep this particular conversation private, "there's a cheesesteak sub in the fridge if you're hungry."

The boy's eyes lit up. "Thanks, Ana." She waited until he loped off into the other room.

"You just did your I-Dream-of-Jeannie thing, didn't you?" Matt asked, the smile evident in his voice, correctly guessing Ana just added one of Derrick's favorite snacks to her refrigerator.

Ana sniffed. "I thought it might be better to speak in private."

She heard a soul-deep sigh through the receiver and pictured Matt running his large hand through his hair, turning it into that slightly messy look that looked so darn sexy on him. Sometimes she thought he did it purposely to draw her attention to the symphony of muscles rippling and flexing in the process. It always worked.

"They all know how I feel about you, Ana."

"You want to protect me. Because of what I did for Dani."

"Ana," he chastised softly. "It's more than that and you know it."

"No, I don't, and neither do you. "

"Ana—"

"No, listen to me. I'll admit that there is...something there. I'm just not sure what it is."

"I can tell you what it is," he said, his voice lowering and becoming all growly, forcing Ana to squeeze her inner thighs together.

"I know what you *think* it is, but I don't even know what I am, and you're—"

"Ana. Stop. We'll work it out together, okay? Slowly. I promise." Matt exhaled again and changed the subject. "Now, tell me why you're suddenly screening your calls. Did I upset you that much?"

Yes. No. Maybe. It was partially him — the dangerous, forbidden feelings he'd stoked earlier — but there was no need to tell him that. Now that he and his muscles and his pheromones weren't there to confuse her, things seemed clearer.

"I'm not upset. I just..." *had an erotic dream about a vampire and then heard his voice in my head* "...couldn't sleep. Just like you said."

She was met with several long moments of silence. There was no way of knowing if he believed her, but there was little he could do about it. The fact that he'd called instead of coming over himself told her he still intended to keep his distance for the time being. That was probably a good thing.

"All right, Ana. Try to get some rest. Derrick and Cal are keeping an eye on things till dawn."

"That's really not necessary."

"We'll have to agree to disagree on that," Matt told her firmly, informing her in no uncertain terms, that he would not budge on this. "Goodnight, Ana. Don't let them schmooze you out of all your food."

* * *

Vlane felt a sudden, violent surge rip through him. It was such a foreign feeling, it took him several minutes to determine what it was: Fear. Terror. Panic.

It had been fleeting, lasting only for the briefest of moments, but it had been real.

Fear was something Vlane had not felt in a long time. As a master vampire, he had reached the stage where such a thing was wholly unnecessary. With his incredible strength, speed, and skill at practically any and all forms of combat, there were few who could hope to challenge him. When he factored in his ability to hypnotize and sway the minds of those who might wish to do him harm, it became even less of an issue.

Obviously, it was not his own fear that rent so viciously through him. It had come and gone in the mere blink of an eye, for no apparent reason. He stood on his patio, gazing out into the lighted gardens, surrounded by nothing but peace and serenity — his own personal turmoil excluded, of course.

So, whose fear had he felt so keenly?

He reached out and touched the minds of those closely connected to him. Armand was in the study, reading. Kristoff was in one of the guest rooms with three human females — pleasuring one with his mouth, one with his hands, and one with his cock.

Jason was checking the perimeter while Zarek replenished his strength in the kitchen.

One by one, he touched upon each of those in his bloodline and found them all to be peacefully engaged in whatever they were doing.

Vlane frowned. Had it been, perhaps, some long forgotten bond reconnecting? While Vlane had always been a responsible sire, there were those who had chosen to go on their own. Was one of them in danger now? It was unlikely. The sensation had passed and he felt no further tug upon his blood bonds.

He tried to recall what he'd been thinking when he'd first felt it. Ah, yes. The fragile female dressed as a lovely faerie who had so captured his attention...

And then, just like that, he knew whose fear he'd sensed. It had been *hers*...

He reached out desperately again, but found nothing. No fear. No panic. Nothing, except perhaps the slightest hint of familiarity. Of recognition.

The realization hit him like the proverbial brick upside the head.

He had *bonded* with the female.

Chapter 9: Under Watchful Eyes

Ana shook her head as brute after brute carried in supplies, stocking the cupboards, pantry, and refrigerator. When she asked them what they were doing, they just grinned and told her to take it up with the Alpha. Ana planned on doing just that, but it would have to wait. She had a full day of appointments and she was already running behind. Lack of sleep coupled with sexual frustration had a way of doing that to a girl.

Dani arrived in the midst of it all, glowing with approval as she viewed the massive quantities of food. Although female and significantly smaller than the males in the pack, Dani managed to eat as much in one day as Ana did in a week. The she-wolf once told Ana Were metabolisms ran much higher than a human's and shifting alone required a tremendous amount of energy.

She greeted the brutes with grins and high-fives, slinging what appeared to be an overnight bag onto one of the oversized sofas in the living space. Ana took one look at the bag and gazed at Dani questioningly. "More food?"

"Hardly," Dani laughed. "I was hoping you'd let me crash on your couch for a couple of days."

Ana narrowed her eyes suspiciously. "Why?"

"Matt's being an overbearing, testosterone-fueled, unreasonable jerk."

Ana hid the twitch of her lips. "He won't let you go on the overnight, huh?" she guessed. Every year a bunch of the young adults took a road trip into the mountains. From what she understood, it was a pretty wild time. She wasn't at all surprised Matt didn't want his little sister going along.

"No," Dani said with a pout that could have rivaled the best Hollywood starlet's. "Maybe next year, when you're finished with school," she mimicked, deepening her voice in an attempt to capture Matt's growly baritone.

Ana held her hand up to her mouth to stifle her giggles. Dani had her brother's stern glare and growly voice down perfectly.

"He says I'm too young, but Jackie — you know, the sleek black one? — gets to go. She's only a couple of months older than me, but then, she's also already let half the males in the pack mount her."

Several of the young brutes unpacking the boxes of groceries bumped knuckles and chuckled at that, causing Dani to glare at them. "Don't you smirk like that, Markus. That's nothing to be proud of. Even your little brother lifted that tail."

Markus's smile faded, but the others laughed. Dani sighed. "Sometimes I hate being the Alpha's sister. No one's got the guts to even try to hit on me like that."

Ana saw Dani glance pointedly at Derrick, who stopped laughing immediately and turned bright red. In the next moment, he was walking purposefully out for more boxes.

Ana didn't pretend to understand everything about adolescent Weres, but from where she stood, they didn't seem all that different from human teenagers. They were more open about things in general, especially their sexuality, and tended to heed their natural instincts, but the underlying premises were the same. There was still that awkward adjustment period when they were no longer children but not quite adults.

"Is that what you want, Dani? To be like Jackie?"

Dani exhaled heavily. "No, not really. But I'm still pissed. So, can I stay?"

Ana didn't have the heart to say no. "I suppose so." Just that quickly, Dani's mood shifted and she was back to grinning. She jumped up and was wrapping Ana in an enthusiastic hug when Matt appeared.

"Dani."

"Uh-oh," Dani whispered loudly in Ana's ear. "Busted."

"I should have known I'd find you here." Matt fixed her with a gimlet eye. "Go on home now and let Ana be."

Dani sniffed, shifting so Ana was between her

and her brother. It was kind of funny, really, because Dani was a full head taller than Ana. "Ana said I could stay."

"Did she now?" Matt turned his Alpha gaze her way. It softened slightly, but not nearly enough. Ana felt herself wilting. So did everyone else in the immediate vicinity as they stopped what they were doing to listen.

Ana took a deep breath to steel herself, her body quivering under the Alpha's authority. Dani gave her arms a squeeze of encouragement.

"Yes," Ana managed in a rather small voice. "I mean, I'd like the company." Matt narrowed his eyes, and Ana hastened to add, "If that's okay with you, of course."

After several long moments, he exhaled. "Fine. Maybe you can teach her how a young female *should* act when surrounded by a bunch of rutting males."

Ana blinked, stunned, not knowing quite how to respond to that. *How would I know?*

She was saved from having to say anything when Matt turned and directed his attention to the young males still hauling in supplies.

"Thanks for standing up for me, Ana," Dani said later as she painted her toenails a sparkly metallic bronze that complimented her natural coloring beautifully. "I think you are quite possibly the only female Matt will listen to when he's in one of his snits."

Ana looked up from the book she was reading, a paranormal romance based on, of all things, werewolves and vampires. At that point, she wasn't sure which one she was rooting for. "He cares about you, Dani."

"Yeah, I know." She glanced at Ana with a wicked grin. "He cares for you, too."

Ana blushed a dark red and tried to hide behind her book. "Of course he does. He cares for everyone around here."

"But you're special."

"No, I'm not." Surely, Matt wouldn't have said anything to Dani. He'd promised.

"Come off it, Ana. My brother's got it bad for you. Jeez, I can still smell the mating scent he left behind."

Without thinking, Ana lifted her face and sniffed lightly. It was faint, but she could smell it — musky, male, and decidedly sensual. She recognized it immediately as the same scent she noticed whenever Matt was nearby.

"Oh, I know that look," laughed Dani. "It's the same look a deer has when it's surrounded and knows it's about to go down."

Ana blinked, trying to regain some semblance of personal control. In that moment, Dani's analogy felt eerily accurate.

"I don't know why you don't just sleep with

him already. Were males are way better than human guys. They're bigger, thicker, and can last all night." It was Dani's turn to blush. "Or, at least, that's what I've heard."

Ana had no intention of discussing her overactive female hormones with Dani, but since she brought it up… "I'm sure lots of she-wolves are willing to…uh, be with your brother."

"Oh, yeah. But he's not serious about any of them. It's like what we were talking about before with Jackie. He'll fuck them, but he won't mate them or chance impregnating them." Ana winced at Dani's explicit language, but the she-wolf didn't appear to notice. "He wants a real mate for that. And from where I'm sniffing, he wants you."

Ana shook her head, her mind and body scrambling to process that little bit of TMI while trying to pull-off the same air of casual comfort Dani had. She was only partially successful. The thought of a male like Matt being interested in her was a heady one indeed, but it also scared her senseless.

"But I'm not a Were, Dani," she countered. "It doesn't make any sense why he would be interested in me. Especially if he wants kids…uh, pups. I mean, I'm not even sure I could…" Her cheeks reddened again when she realized she was actually thinking out loud.

"He could turn you," Dani said quietly. "Didn't he offer?"

"Yes, he did, but that was only so he could offer his protection." Wasn't it? He didn't make the offer until after he found out what Vlane Masterson had done.

"Don't kid yourself. Matt wouldn't have offered such a thing for something he could give you anyway. And Weres can breed with human females as easily as they can she-wolves. Easier, really, because human fertility cycles occur every month compared to the less frequent heat cycle for us. No, Ana. If all Matt cared about was siring pups, he could have had dozens by now. Not too many bitches would say no to a piece of that, you know?"

Ana thought about that for a while. Yes, she knew. Even she felt the persistent tug of his pheromone-fueled spell whenever he was around. Ruggedly handsome, oozing barely-leashed power and male sexuality, Matt might have just walked around with a big sign that said, "come on, you know you want to". But how much of that was a purely physical reaction, based solely in biochemistry and the hard-wired primitive urge to mate with the strongest male? Sure, the sex would probably be phenomenally hot, but could it ever be anything more than that?

"I think he might have changed his mind anyway. He's been avoiding me the past few days," Ana said finally. Other than brief, cameo appearances like the one earlier, Matt hadn't been by much since he'd almost marked her in the kitchen.

Ana wasn't quite sure how she felt about that. His notable absence both relieved and vexed her. On the one hand, it simplified things. She didn't have to worry about her involuntary (and confusing) hormonally-based reactions to him when he wasn't around. On the other hand, she kind of missed him. Alpha power aside, Matt was a very likable, personable kind of guy. And the only one who knew her secret.

Ana exhaled heavily, conflicted. Surely she must be sending out mixed signals if she couldn't even resolve her own feelings.

Dani bit her lip, as if deciding whether to say something. After a long moment, she finally said, "Ana, there's something you must understand about Were males. When a female goes into her mating heat, it's nearly impossible for the males to resist, especially if they have feelings for the female to begin with. For she-wolves who aren't interested in mating, it's not a big deal. We only hit our heat cycles twice a year, and for those couple of days, we just make ourselves scarce or hole up somewhere so we don't tempt the males."

Dani paused, shooting Ana an uncomfortable glance. "I don't really know if there's a right way to tell you this, so I'm just going to say it, okay? Matt's trying to stay away from you because you are fertile right now and it's driving him nuts. It's one of the reasons his mating scent is so strong in here — he's using it to mask your scent from the others. All they can smell is him."

"But *you* know," Ana said, her words barely audible. She felt as if she were on the verge of total mortification.

"Because I'm a female," Dani said logically. "Females have a better sense of smell."

Oh. "Should I leave for a few days?"

"No," Dani answered, but her tone lacked conviction. "I suggested that, but Matt shot me down. He wants both of us to stay close by. I'm not sure why, exactly."

"I'm sure he has his reasons," Ana offered. And she was pretty sure she knew what they were.

"Yeah," Dani agreed, "but it's still a pain in the butt. I don't think he'd object to a small road trip to Bransonville, though. It's the closest thing we have to a big city around here, only about a two hour drive. We can make a day of it! I need some stuff, and it would be nice to have another girl's opinion. We could have lunch there, maybe get our hair and nails done. What do you say?"

Dani looked so hopeful Ana didn't have the heart to turn her down. And maybe a day away from Mythic would help her clear her head and sort out her thoughts.

"I'll check the schedule, but I think it's pretty light tomorrow. A couple of early morning check-ups, nothing major. As long as someone's here to page me if an emergency comes in, it should be doable."

Satisfied, Dani stifled a yawn and made a nest for herself on the sofa. "Awesome."

Chapter 10: Well, That Was Unexpected

There were only a few events that resulted in a blood bond between a vampire and another being. The first involved turning a human or other inferior creature into a blood slave. Vampire blood could have an intoxicating effect upon those who drank it, and if ingested often enough, was as addicting as modern day heroin or methamphetamine. In exchange for "fixes", the blood slave agreed to some level of servitude. The longer the agreement continued, the more dependent the recipient became. As a result, the period of said indenture usually lasted for the remainder of the creature's natural lifespan.

The second was obvious – when a vampire sired another by draining his or her blood and then replacing it with his own. That was a lifelong commitment, and one taken very seriously by his kind since their lifespan could continue indefinitely.

The first method involved no death and small exchanges of blood over an extended period of time. The second involved death and a massive exchange of blood. Neither applied in this situation.

Which left a third possibility that nearly brought him to his knees: he had met his true, fated mate.

It was such a rare occurrence that he hadn't even considered it. In the case of true, fated mates, a dormant bond snapped into effect with only the slightest interaction and exchange of bodily fluid. It could be something as simple as a kiss... or the single bite of a vampire upon the one the Fates had chosen for him and him alone.

It was a staggering thought. After five centuries, was it possible he had finally crossed paths with the one who would complete him? Or was this, like his temporary return to mortality, some kind of cruel trick?

He briefly considered sending Kristoff, Jason, or Zarek to her as a precautionary test. If one of them bit her and experienced the same strange phenomenon he had, he rationalized, then he would know that something unnatural and devious was afoot. He nixed that idea almost immediately. Just the thought of another male partaking of Ana filled him with a surge of possessive rage.

One thing was certain: Vlane *would* find out, and sooner rather than later. With that in mind, he set off to find his ancient friend and trusted advisor. If there was anyone familiar with the rare phenomenon of fated mates, it would be Armand.

Vlane had been trying to "reach" Ana all day. He sent out discreet, tiny pulses, not wanting to alarm her unnecessarily or alert her to his presence. The more he thought about it, the more it seemed she could hear him, but was able to erect some kind of barrier that prevented him from hearing her.

He had never heard of such a thing, but then again, he had never come across a creature like her before, either. He had no idea what she was capable of, beyond the ability to make him human, that was. He decided his best strategy was to attempt to make a connection with her while she was sleeping, when she was most vulnerable. Her resistance would be at its weakest, and he might be able to push into her mind.

He was in his private suite, atop the ridiculously large bed when he was finally able to achieve a connection. With his hands folded over his abdomen, he closed his eyes and focused his power, gently reaching out to her. Almost immediately, images assaulted him. His cock grew hard and heavy, and his normally-dormant heart began to stutter erratically. He had made it past her impressive mental shields and into her mind and she was having erotic dreams.

Of him.

And her.

Together.

He could see the images in vivid detail; as one, his senses grabbed onto them and took on a life of their own. In her dream, he covered her body with his own, pounding into her with deliberate purpose and intention. He *felt* her tight sheath strangling his cock. *Tasted* the sweet flesh of her generous breasts. Filled his lungs with her fresh, living scent made stronger by the heat of her arousal. Heard the breathy, guttural moans rising up from within the deepest parts of her soul.

He moved deeper. Harder. Faster. The *need* to be inside her was all-consuming.

It still wasn't enough. He lifted his head as her body bucked and seized beneath him in yet another explosive release, knowing if he drank of her now, her blood would have the potency of a star turning supernova. His fangs extended, his head reared back, and he struck with the speed of a cobra, burying his fangs in her neck as he buried his cock deep in her channel, filling her with his seed while taking her life's blood into him.

Ana, he moaned, draining her as she drained him.

* * *

Ana woke with a start, shooting into an upright, sitting position. She was covered in sweat, her hair plastered to her face and neck. Gasping for breath, body shaking, her hand went to her belly where an explosive tingling was still radiating through her core. Only after several deep, cleansing breaths did it begin to subside.

She had become somewhat accustomed to the erotic dreams, but they had never been like *that*. So real. So vivid. She was pretty certain she actually orgasmed.

Ana. She heard the voice in her head, a sensual moan that intensified the lingering tingles. *Come to me, Ana.*

No! She answered reflexively. Her heart continued to pound; her head swam, dazed and confused by the unusually intense sensations.

You must. You belong to me, little Ana. Come, and I will show you the reality of your dreams.

No! Leave me alone.

A quiet, determined, and very male chuckle suffused with power echoed in her mind. *Never...*

Ana slammed down her mental walls, cutting him off. She got out of bed, tossed off her sweat-soaked nightclothes, and pulled a cool, dry nightshirt over her head.

He knew who she was. And he knew about the connection.

What the hell was she going to do now?

* * *

Vlane was shaken. He opened his eyes after the little vixen so thoroughly shut him out, aghast that he had just ejaculated all over himself. Her dream had been so real, so vivid, it had actually brought him to completion. *The last time he'd had a wet dream*, he thought wryly as he got up to clean himself, *was about five hundred years ago, when he had been a twelve year old human boy.*

It was every bit as humiliating now as it had been then.

But it hadn't been for nothing. Now, he knew for certain he had unknowingly created a bond with her that night. It wasn't a very strong bond, though. She had been able to shut him out easily enough once she realized what was happening. Only a drop or two of his venom must have been released before he lost consciousness. Either that, or she was far more powerful than he had given her credit for.

It didn't matter. Weak or not, there *was* a bond between them. And, he thought, as he continued to wipe his abdomen, his copious disgrace illustrated one very important fact: he had to have her.

Chapter 11: So Much For Keeping Secrets

"Ana? What are you doing?" Dani asked sleepily with a yawn as she padded into the kitchen.

"Getting some warm milk. I'm sorry I woke you."

"S'okay. Weres are notoriously light sleepers. Can't sleep, huh?"

Ana shook her head.

"It's your body trying to tell you something, you know. You should listen. Hook-up with my brother. It'll get him off the rag and he'll have you so exhausted, you'll sleep for days."

Ana sighed, pulling the milk out of the microwave and stirring in some vanilla and sugar. A few residual tingles sparked up occasionally, but mostly, she just felt spent. Is this what it would be like if she gave in to her body's lustful urges? If not for the whole terrifying I've-bonded-with-a-vampire mental aspect, it might not be so bad. Then again, Dani wasn't talking about Vlane Masterson. Things would be even more complicated with Matt.

She handed the mug to Dani and began to make

another for herself. "I don't think it's that simple, Dani."

"Sure it is. He's a male. You're a female. You're both obviously hot and bothered by each other. What's the problem?"

"He said something about marking me."

Dani's eyes grew big. "Wow. Are you sure?"

Ana nodded. She didn't know much about the process, but she was pretty sure it went way beyond conversion or even sex. Marking had to do with ownership, and that was some serious stuff. Granted, it would provide a means of protection against the scary vampire haunting her dreams (no matter how erotic they were, he still terrified her), but that was no basis for a *marking.* And as much as she liked Matt and found him incredibly attractive, she just wasn't ready for that.

Besides, how could she allow one man to mark her while she consistently dreamt of another?

"Wow."

"Yeah."

"Are you going to let him?"

Ana shook her head.

"Why not? I'm mean, you like him, don't you?"

"Yes, very much. But I'm not ready for that level of commitment, and I'm not convinced he'd be doing it for the right reasons."

Dani thought about this, her youthful brow drawn into the slightest of furrows. "You think it's some misplaced sense of gratitude for what you did for me?"

"Maybe." It could be that, but it could be many things. Ana had considered them all, time and time again. The reasons covered a wide spectrum of possibilities, the most harmless being a mutual, physical attraction clamoring for completion. Another suggested she was nothing more than a pawn in an ancient pissing contest between the two races (she blamed that paranormal romance for breathing life into that particular idea).

The worst embraced her biggest fear: Matt wanted her for reasons that had everything to do with her unique abilities and nothing to do with *her*. She didn't want to believe Matt was capable of such a thing; in fact, he had never given any kind of indication he was anything but honest about his feelings, but Ana had seen too much "unintentional" greed to completely stifle the niggling doubt.

"There's more to it, though, isn't there?" Dani said, wrenching her back from her wandering thoughts. "You haven't told me everything."

"No," Ana admitted wearily. In her current state, she didn't have the strength to craft a clever, misdirecting response. Nor could she deny it outright, either, because of that pesky inability to lie. The past two weeks had taken their toll. After hardly being able to sleep or eat, constantly battling against feelings and needs she had no idea how to fight, Ana was desperately tired, both mentally and physically. "Something happened. The night of the masquerade ball."

"I knew it! You've been acting weird since you went. Come on, sister. Spill it."

Ana bit her lip and shook her head. "I don't think that's such a good idea." She already regretted telling Matt. Not that he had abused her confidence in any way, but it had changed something between them.

It always did, she thought sadly. No matter how much anyone said it didn't matter, having that kind of knowledge changed the way you looked at things. Whoever had said ignorance was bliss was wise beyond words.

"Like I'm giving you a choice." Dani let a low warning growl escape.

Even though she believed Dani would never intentionally hurt her, Ana couldn't fully suppress the deep-seated, instinctual warning to flee. Yes, Dani was a young, beautiful woman Ana counted among her limited friends, but she was also a very deadly, very capable predator. Ana would do well to remember that.

"You know I have a whole drawer full of tranquilizing darts in the next room, don't you?" Ana asked, only half-joking. She just wasn't sure whether it would be better to use them on Dani or herself.

"Just try to make a run for it. See how far you get."

For some bizarre reason she might never understand, Ana did just that. She swiveled on the counter stool and hit the ground running. She barely made it out of the room before a solid weight of sleek muscle and fur hit her, pushing her onto the couch. In her wolf form, Dani sat her haunches on the backs of Ana's legs and used her forepaws to press down upon her shoulder blades. Then, Ana felt the rasp of Dani's tongue along the back of her arm.

Ana laughed into the sofa cushions. Dani's tongue tickled. "Okay, okay. You win. I give."

A heartbeat later, Dani's long, bronzed legs were straddling Ana's back and she was laughing. "Damn, Ana. You *do* taste good. Salty, but sweet. No wonder all the males want to lick you."

"Get off!" Ana laughed, trying to buck under Dani's solid weight. Dani slid off and allowed Ana to sit up. The she-wolf smoothed her hair, doing nothing to conceal the smug, triumphant gleam in her eye.

"You really are a bitch, Dani," Ana said, smiling.

"And don't you forget it." The young Were smirked. "Now, come on. You can tell me what's got your panties in a twist in the kitchen. I'm starving."

"Okay. I'll tell you. But it goes no farther, agreed?"

Dani thought for a moment. "As long as what

you tell me doesn't hurt my brother, I agree."

It was the most she could hope for under the circumstances. Ana took a deep breath and readied herself. "So, you know I went to the after party, right? Well, what I didn't tell you was…"

"Holy shit, Ana," Dani said a long while later, a veritable feast laid out before her to both prove Ana's incredible story and sate her hunger. "I can't believe you were holding out on me." She shook her head. "All this time, all the good things that have been happening lately, it has been because of you?"

Ana shifted in her seat. "Not all of it."

"So, when I totally rocked those SATs, that was your doing?"

"No," Ana said emphatically. "That was all you. I just gave you an extra push to keep you calm and focused so you didn't panic. You knew all that stuff, you just lacked the confidence to believe you could do it."

"And when that big company upriver that was dumping all that stuff illegally suddenly closed down and went out of business…?"

Ana looked into her mug. "Some shredded and incriminating documents *may* have been reformed and ended up in the hands of a couple of key officials and reporters known for their green policies."

"And Sasha's unexpected letter from the family

she thought perished in those earthquakes when she was just a baby?"

Ana's eyes glistened, but she said nothing.

"What about the high rate of matings and healthy litters we've had over the past couple of months?"

"I can't create something from nothing, Dani," Ana said, squirming uncomfortably. "I can only work with what's already there."

Dani gaped at her in wonder. "You're like a faerie godmother."

Ana looked wholly embarrassed. "Your brother called me a genie."

"He knows?" Understanding began to dawn in Dani's eyes.

"Yeah. He's the only one beside you." Ana grew serious. "But no one else can, Dani. I trust you, and I trust Matt, but that kind of knowledge changes people."

"You think Matt wants you because of what you can do."

Did she? Despite the lingering doubt that would always be there — no, she didn't really believe that. If it were anybody else, maybe. But it would be pretty smart on his part if that were the case. Matt knew she cared deeply for the pack, and as the Alpha's mate, that bond would only grow. Who wouldn't want someone with her abilities looking out for their pack?

Aside from being gorgeous and caring, Matt

was also incredibly intelligent. While it was likely that he had carefully considered the benefits of selecting her, she didn't think that was the primary reason behind his offer to mark and mate her. Matt would go to great lengths for his pack, but he would consider her needs as well.

"No, I don't think that," Ana replied honestly. Matt did care for her and wanted to protect her, even if she didn't fully understand the depths of those feelings. "I'm just not convinced I'm the best choice for him."

"You're beautiful, Ana. Sweet and smart and caring. You're already taking care of us. Why wouldn't you be?"

"Of course I care about the pack. You've become like family to me. But look at you. You're tall and strong and beautiful. A perfect she-wolf. Everything a normal, healthy male could possibly want in a mate. Now, look at me. I'm nothing like that."

"Don't sell yourself short, Ana. I wasn't kidding when I said there were a lot of males interested in you."

"Because I'm different. A novelty. But I would always be a liability, don't you see? I'm not strong like you, or brave. Even now, Matt feels the need to protect me. Making the pack take turns guarding me. Sending his younger sister over here under the guise of a sibling spat to keep an eye on me."

Dani's eyes widened and Ana smirked. "Yeah,

I knew. Give me some credit, will you?"

"I don't see where any of that's bad," Dani said defensively.

"It's not bad," Ana said gently. "I'm honored and touched that you care for me so much. I really am. Which is exactly why I couldn't bear it if anything happened to you because of me. Anyone who knows anything about me knows how much I care about you and that I'd do anything to keep you safe."

Unlike Matt, Dani did not immediately discount Ana's fears. She was silent for several moments, considering the possibilities. "Vlane Masterson knows, doesn't he?"

"I don't know. He knows *something*, but I'm not sure what or how much. He's managed to connect enough dots to figure out I was the one at the after party that night, and he knows he can speak to me in my thoughts when my guard is down."

Dani's eyes widened again. She was beginning to look more like an owl than a wolf. "Oh, Ana! Have you told Matt?"

"No, and you're not going to tell him either," Ana said firmly. "He'll have me under lock and key if he finds out."

"Yeah, but this is Vlane Masterson we're talking about. He's a powerful vampire."

"Exactly. Which is why you have to let me handle this."

"I can't let you do this alone," Dani insisted, shaking her head. "It's too dangerous."

Ana looked at Dani, deep into her stubborn golden brown eyes, so like her brother's. Of course it would come to this. She had known it would. Maybe that's why she shared her secrets with Dani —because inwardly, she knew they would wind up here.

She reached her hand out and cupped the side of the girl's face gently. She knew what she had to do. "I know, Dani. You are a good friend."

"Thanks, Ana. Don't worry. We'll figure something out."

Ana already had. She let the magic build slowly inside of her. "For your safety, I wish for you to forget I told you about my gift," she said softly. "That you forget everything I told you about Vlane Masterson. About what transpired the night of the after party and since. That you know how glad I am to have you in my life and you can come to me any time to talk about school, boys, your overbearing brother, and all the other things you're dealing with right now."

Ana pulled her hand away slowly and sat back. Dani blinked, her eyes somewhat sleepy and dazed. Then, she yawned.

"I'm sorry, Ana. I think that warm vanilla milk thing really did the trick. Thanks for letting me unload on you."

"Anytime, Dani," Ana said with a serene smile

as she gathered their mugs and put them in the sink. "I'm always here for you."

* * *

Vlane paced the length of his private lair. For the first time in a very long time, he did not know how to proceed.

There was no doubt now that Ana was aware of his repeated attempts to connect with her, but even the slightest brush against her mind was now met with extreme resistance. While it frustrated him, it intrigued him as well. Finally, he'd found a woman worthy of making an effort.

He did so enjoy a challenge.

Chapter 12: Ready or Not...

Dani rolled her eyes, gripping the can of soda while Matt gave her the third degree. She hadn't been back in their house two minutes before he sat her down at the kitchen table and began the interrogation. "Honestly. We *talked*."

"Derrick said the lights were on from two a.m. to five a.m.! What could you possibly talk about for three hours?"

"Girl stuff. Jeez, Matt. No wonder Ana's freaked out. You have her under constant surveillance."

Matt flinched. "She's really freaked out?"

"Wouldn't you be?" Dani asked. "She's got big hairy wolves breathing down her neck every time she turns around, watching her every move, sniffing at her like she's some kind of juicy snack."

His features hardened. "Who's sniffing her?"

Dani rolled her eyes again. She had it down to an art form. That, combined with the smirk she gave him, reminded him she-wolves could be every bit as cunning as the males.

"Chill, Alpha-brother. There's only one wolf that's captured her interest."

"Yeah?" he asked, unable to hide all of the hope he felt at his sister's words.

"Yeah, but you're scaring her, I think," Dani said, softening a little. "She's not like us, Matt."

He exhaled heavily and his shoulders slumped. "I know." Man, did he know. He scratched the back of his neck, feeling the frustration of that fact. "I don't know much about" – Matt caught himself before he said 'genies' – "human females."

"You don't know much about females, period," Dani shot back, but it was a gentle stab. "Are you courting her?"

"I'm *protecting* her," Matt clarified. "Keeping her safe, making sure she has everything she needs."

"That's great, if you're her pack leader or her boss. But if you want to be more than that, that's not going to cut it."

"So, what are you saying? I should buy her flowers? Take her out to dinner? That kind of thing?" The thought of such things was enough to give him a rash. She-wolves were much less complicated. Courting among Weres was a simple, straightforward process. When a male was interested in a female as a mate, he let her know by proving himself worthy with a show of strength, skill, and physical attributes. Easy.

But somehow, Matt didn't think beating the snot out of other eligible males vying for her attention and then mounting her in a victory claiming would impress Ana.

"It would be a good start. Maybe she'll begin to see you as more than the guy who feels indebted to her."

"Christ. Is that what she thinks?"

Dani shrugged. "Ana's hard to figure out, even for me. But I do know I really like her. And I want her to stick around."

Matt's head snapped up. "What do you mean? Did she say something about leaving?"

Dani bit her lip. "Not exactly, no. Call it intuition. I just have this feeling she's going to bolt."

He stood up and puffed out his chest. "She can't do that."

"Yes, Matt, she can," she said quietly. "She doesn't belong to you. And…something's just not right."

"Dani, if you know something, you have to tell me."

"I can't. It's more like a feeling than actual knowledge. Like, there's something I *should* know but just can't quite grasp. The more I try to think about it, the farther away it gets."

It was frustrating as hell. Matt was a wolf, goddammit, and the Alpha. But pushing Dani wasn't going to get them anywhere constructive. He blew out a heavy breath and ran his hands over his face. "All right. I think you should continue to stay with her for a while. Keep an eye on things."

"She's going to figure it out, Matt. She's not going to buy this teenage angst thing forever."

"I know." He just didn't know what else to do.

* * *

Ana tugged off her plastic gloves and dropped them in the waste container. "Chauncey's heart is working too hard, Mrs. Conroy," she said bluntly. "If he doesn't lose some weight and start exercising, he's not going to see his next birthday."

She wasn't normally quite so direct, but she had a soft spot for the little Dachshund. He had big, soulful eyes and a gentle temperament. He was only four years old. He should have a lot of life left in him, but at nearly three times his healthy body weight, the poor guy was suffering.

"He likes his treats," Mrs. Conroy sniffed. She looked like she was a couple times her healthy weight, too. The glare she gave Ana suggested someone as small as her couldn't possibly begin to understand.

"Of course he does. But he's hurting, Mrs. Conroy. And he's not opening the cupboards and treating himself, now is he?"

The woman opened her mouth to say something, but Ana halted her. "I know you love Chauncey and you want to spoil him, but maybe you could do so in healthier ways?"

"Like what?" the woman asked cautiously.

"Well, there's a great program in town where people take their dogs for an hour or so each day. There's a heated swimming pool there. He could get some exercise without putting any undue stress on his joints. Then, when he loses a few pounds, you could enroll him in a doggie play group."

"A play group?"

"Yes. He'd get to socialize with other dogs around his size and temperament. I believe several of the owners get together and have coffee or take a walk around the park. It might be fun for both of you."

Mrs. Conroy seemed to consider it. Ana didn't know too much about her, but she did know Mrs. Conroy was a widow who lived on the outskirts of town and generally kept to herself.

Ana took a business card from the counter and wrote on it. "Here's the number. There's usually a waiting list, but Jake — the guy who owns it — is a good guy. Tell him Doc Ana sent you and he'll arrange for a tour so you can decide if it might be something you and Chauncey want to try."

She still seemed unsure. "You say it will help Chauncey?"

"Without a doubt."

"Okay."

"Great! How about we schedule a three-month follow-up, no charge, to see how he's doing?"

"Okay." Mrs. Conroy seemed particularly brightened by the no charge offer.

"And here's a list of healthy snacks for when he's giving you the hungry eyes," she smiled, ruffling Chauncey's ears. He gave her a big doggie grin in response.

Ana heaved a sigh of relief as she wiped down the exam table. Dani wouldn't be back for another couple hours, and the ever-present guard around the Sanctuary seemed to have let up a little, at least during business hours. The way she figured it, she had a whole hour to herself.

Or so she'd thought. No sooner had she put everything away then the jingle of the front door sounded, announcing another visitor.

Oh, well. She didn't really want that cup of tea anyway. And it was probably better to wait until later tonight to pick up that book again. Once she did, it was so hard to put down, and the girl in the story was just about to make up her mind between the vampire and the werewolf. Ana wasn't sure which one she was rooting for.

She emerged from the back to greet whoever it was, forcing a pleasant and welcoming smile to her face. That smile froze, however, when she realized who it was that stood before her.

A tall man, she judged him to be at least six-two, lean and nicely proportioned. Late twenties, or thereabouts, with blue-black hair, perfect, pale skin, and piercing, jet-black eyes.

Vlane Masterson.

* * *

Vlane stared at the tiny female. He didn't remember her being quite so small. Then again, she had probably been wearing heels that night, and the fullness of her gown had given the illusion of someone a bit more...substantial. Her golden hair was pulled back into a ponytail, her face devoid of makeup. She looked more like a girl than a woman, especially in those ridiculous clothes. His lips quirked as he looked her up and down, taking in the dancing cartoon cows adorning her formless top.

For a moment, he thought he must have the wrong woman. There was no way this tiny little thing held the kind of power he had felt that night. Then he looked into her eyes and saw the brilliant clarity, intelligence, and most importantly, recognition.

Oh, yes. She was the one he wanted. His body tingled at the knowledge.

"Dr. McKinnon?" His voice was deep and smooth, intentionally hypnotic.

"Y-Yes," she stammered, clearing her throat nervously.

Vlane offered what he hoped was a friendly smile. He could scent her fear. The last thing he wanted was to scare her away. Or for her to call for her wolf guard. The tiny silver whistle hung from a thin chain around her neck. He had no doubt she would use it if she felt threatened, and he had no wish to break the tenuous truce between his people and the Weres unnecessarily.

"I must apologize. I do not have an appointment, but perhaps you may fit us in?"

Chapter 13: It Just Got Real

Until that moment, Ana hadn't noticed the cat he held in his arms. With its silky black fur, it blended perfectly into the black of his shirt and slacks. Silvery-golden eyes with a hint of red, the exact color of a spectacular blood moon, blinked lazily at her.

"Oh, of course. Would you like to bring her back?" Instinctively, she knew the feline was female by the utterly contented look on its face. Ana had a feeling most women would feel the same way in Vlane Masterson's arms. The man had a magnetic pull to rival the poles; even Ana found herself fighting the inclination to close the distance between them.

He followed her so silently, she had to look over her shoulder to confirm he was even there.

Breathe, Ana, she commanded herself, nearly closing her eyes when her lungs filled with his rich, dark scent. She was trembling again, but not wholly out of fear. Tingles of awareness skittered along her skin. It was the exact same reaction she'd had the night of the after party, as if all of her senses had just suddenly come alive with his nearness.

"Would you like to put her on the exam table, or would you prefer to hold her?"

"I will hold her, if you do not mind."

"Whatever makes you more comfortable," Ana answered with a little smile, but inwardly, her heart was pounding a mile a minute. His deep voice resonated along her auditory nerves and to examine the cat, she'd have to get close to him, too.

Of course, that was probably exactly what he'd intended.

"She's beautiful," Ana commented. The cat looked at her and blinked, acknowledging the statement as nothing less than truth. "Is she having a problem, or is this just a check-up?" Ana asked.

"I was hoping you could tell me," Vlane said smoothly. "Bast has been rather unsettled as of late."

It figured his cat would have the name of an ancient Egyptian goddess. "Unsettled?"

Vlane nodded, his shining obsidian eyes boring into her as she stepped between his knees to examine the feline. The cat let out a loud purr when Ana stroked her back.

"You have quite a way with animals, Dr. McKinnon," Vlane said, a bit of surprise lacing his tone. "Bast does not tolerate strangers well — especially females."

Ana wasn't sure how to respond to that. Was it a compliment? Or a warning?

"Have you noticed any changes in her

behavior? Her eating habits?"

"She eats, but she is not satisfied. She rests, yet she cannot find peace." The words wrapped around her like a lovely, haunting melody. So familiar. So…appropriate. Ana could definitely relate.

She pressed the stethoscope gently to the cat, hoping he didn't see her hands shaking or hear her heart pounding like a jackhammer against the walls of her chest. She took her time, focusing as much attention as she could on the animal while fighting the urge to touch *him*.

"She seems fine now."

"That is because she is where she belongs. With me. In my arms. It is where she finds that which she truly needs."

That voice, it slipped inside her, caressed the most feminine parts of her until she felt the urge to purr, too. Finding it hard to breathe, she took a step back. When had it gotten so hot?

"Well," she said, drawing away with some effort. "She seems to be in perfect health, Mr., uh…" She paused, wondering if it would be wise to reveal she knew his name. He hadn't openly recognized her, either.

"Masterson," he said. "Vlane Masterson. I believe you attended an event at my estate several weeks ago."

"Ah, yes, of course," she said, feeling the heat rise in her cheeks.

"And declined my subsequent request for

dinner." He smiled patiently while Bast looked at her with undisguised curiosity, as if she couldn't figure out for the life of her why Ana would refuse such an invitation. "Would you, perhaps, reconsider?"

Ana turned her back to him to wash her hands at the sink — a rather foolish act, she realized. Wasn't that how all this started in the first place? With him at her back? The memory of his body crowding hers, the feel of his cool breath just before the glorious penetration of his fangs, had the area between her thighs warming and growing increasingly moist.

"I don't think so, Mr. Masterson."

The clock ticked off several seconds of silence. Could he sense her fear? Her arousal? Did he know refusing him was one of the hardest things she'd ever done? And was that his doing — some kind of vampire-mojo mind-body control thing — or hers?

Finally, he spoke. "May I inquire as to why not?"

She hesitated, clutching the small paper towel like a lifeline. She didn't want to answer him. It would reveal too much.

"Why does it matter, Mr. Masterson?" she asked quietly. "Of what interest am I to you?"

He regarded her for so long, she wasn't quite sure he would answer. Those eyes, glittering and black, looked right into her, as if he was trying to figure out the answer to that one himself.

"I failed to properly introduce myself as your host," he said, finally. "It is an unforgivable offense, one I wish to rectify."

"Well, you just have, so we're good. It's very nice to meet you, Mr. Masterson."

Suddenly, he was there, in front of her. She had no idea how he managed to move so quickly, or what had happened to his cat. One exceptionally long, well-manicured finger caught her beneath her chin and lifted her eyes to his. She drew in a breath; it was impossible to look away. Glittering black eyes, infinitely deep, bore into her own. At that moment, she couldn't think of any reason why she would want to look away.

"I did not get to dance with you, Ana," he said, his words a soft caress up and down the length of her spine. "And I so wish to dance with you…"

Her eyes grew heavy and her body began to ache in very specific places. Voices, familiar ones, intruded on her pleasant fog, calling as if from far away.

"Ana! Hey, Doc! You back there?!"

"Tell them you are with a patient," Vlane commanded softly.

"Yeah, I'm with a patient," she called out without breaking eye contact.

"You will be done shortly."

"I'll be out in a bit. Feel free to raid the fridge."

"Cool," one of the boys responded. From the examination room, they heard the brutes moving through the waiting room toward Ana's private living space.

"Come with me, Ana," he breathed, moving even closer.

She wanted to, but something was holding her back. What was holding her back? "I...can't."

"You must," Vlane said, cupping her face, brushing his lips lightly over hers.

His lips were so cool, so very soft. She reached for more, but he pulled back slightly, denying her that which she so craved. "I must?"

"Yes. Just for a little while, Ana. Just one dance."

* * *

Dani dropped her backpack on the kitchen floor and grabbed a Rockstar from the fridge. Because of her high metabolism, the energy drink had no more effect on her than a regular Coke would on a normal teenager. For some reason, the sickeningly sweet taste really appealed to her.

"Where's Ana?" she said, poking her head into the living room. Food covered every available surface and the brutes were knee-deep in a game of Mortal Kombat.

"In the back with a patient," Derrick answered without looking up.

"No, she's not. I was just back there."

Cal looked up and frowned. "She was there

when we got here about fifteen minutes ago. Said she was finishing up and would be out soon."

Dani went out to the reception desk and picked up Ana's appointment book. "Her last appointment was over two hours ago."

"So? Maybe it was a long one."

Dani shook her head. The hair on the back of her neck prickled; something didn't feel right. "No. It was only a checkup. And it was Mrs. Conroy. I saw her in town just a little while ago when I was waiting for the bus."

"A walk-in, maybe?" Cal offered.

The boys put down their controllers and followed Dani into the exam room. It was empty; nothing appeared out of order. Dani walked straight to the other side of the room and pushed open another door to the surgical area. She did that through the entire facility, going from room to room in a big circle until she came back to the waiting room.

"Are you sure she didn't come into the house?"

Derrick and Cal didn't think so, but they checked it out anyway. Kitchen, living room, bedroom, bathroom — nothing. Everything looked as it should.

Her instincts told her that something wasn't right. Dani lifted her nose and sniffed, picking up faint traces of feminine perfume, weiner dog, a feline of indeterminate breed, and something else. *Vampire.*

"I'm calling Matt."

Chapter 14: Into the Vampire's Lair

With only a slight bit of coaxing, Ana had followed him out the Sanctuary's back exit like a docile puppy. She slid into the front seat of his expensive, UV-protected sports car while he held the door open, and sat quietly for the thirty minute drive to his estate with a purring and contented Bast in her lap (a feat which both impressed and befuddled him). She made no protest when he took her hand and led her into his manse, and even accepted a small glass of brandy to calm her nerves once he guided her to his elegant office.

"I shouldn't be here," Ana said softly, more to herself than him, yet she displayed no genuine distress. She had come of her own volition. Mostly. He had only used the slightest hint of compulsion, though he had been prepared to use more if necessary. He probably wouldn't have used even that had the brutes not shown up when they had and forced his hand.

"On the contrary," Vlane said smoothly. "You are exactly where you should be."

"What do you want, Mr. Masterson?" she asked bluntly, turning away from the beveled glass windows to cast her inquisitive gaze upon him. Such a powerful gaze she had. Her faceted green eyes shimmered in the filtered light, reminding him of a rare Tsavorite garnet. The gem was one of his personal favorites, its intense color more brilliant than a fine emerald. Deep in his chest, he felt his dormant heart stutter once, then twice.

"I think we are past such formalities. Please, call me Vlane. And you know what I want, Ana."

Those long, golden lashes fluttered slightly before she blinked. "No. I really don't."

Vlane shook himself free of her mesmerizing eyes, pinning her with a powerful gaze of his own. "Let us begin with the burning question. Why did you make me human?"

Ana gasped, her expression quickly turning to shock. "Is that what happened to you?" she asked. "You don't seem human to me."

"Do not toy with me," he warned. He allowed a bit of his power to radiate around him. "I have been more than accommodating, but my patience quickly wanes. What are you? How do you hold such power over life and death?"

She swallowed, her eyes still wide. Taking a step back, she wrapped her arms around herself and sat down, presumably in an effort to make herself smaller. "I don't know."

Her feeble attempt to claim ignorance was unacceptable. "You made me human!" he roared, pounding his fist on the desk, causing her bottom to lift several inches from the seat. "How does one tiny slip of a human female make a five hundred year old vampire human?"

Tears began to well up in her eyes, her hands wringing in her lap. "I didn't do that. You did."

In a split second, he was inches from her face. "*Do. Not. Lie. To. Me.*"

"I *cannot* lie. It must have been your wish," she sobbed softly. "It was what you desired most when you took my blood."

Vlane stilled, his rage draining with each tear that coursed down her cheek. Amazed, he touched one with his finger and brought it to his lips. The taste burst across his tongue. Fresh. Pure. Brimming with an incomprehensible energy, making him feel... *alive*.

Her words penetrated his haze of temporary euphoria. *It must have been your wish...* Wish. Energy. It wasn't possible. Was it?

"Show me," he demanded.

She shook her head in refusal, her shoulders shuddering with silent sobs. He grabbed her delicate hand and pierced the tip of her finger with his extended fang, effectively taking the choice away from her. He took no pleasure in bullying her, but he needed to know the truth. Was she a consummate actress, a trickster, a danger to him and his kind? Or was her verisimilitude genuine?

He raised her hand to his lips and squeezed a drop onto his tongue with but a single thought: *I wish to know the truth.*

Her blood exploded in a symphony of colors and music within him. He did not collapse like last time; instead, he simply staggered backward as his wish was granted, the truth revealed in startling clarity.

He had heard of such creatures before, but had never actually come across one. Because they had disappeared thousands of years ago, existing now only in myths.

"You are *Faerie*," he said, his voice filled with awe. "But that is impossible!" He pushed her hair away from her ears; they did not have the pointed tips characteristic of the legendary race. He ran his hands down her back, feeling none of the cartilage serving as an anchor for wings.

She continued to cry softly. "I don't know what I am."

Vlane paced back and forth, resisting the overwhelming urge to soothe her; providing comfort to another was something he hadn't done in centuries. The startling truth consumed him. Ana was Faerie, with enough ancient magic to give her the power to make him mortal, if only for a day.

Because *he* had wished it, not because she had.

"You have what you asked for. You know the truth. Will you release me now?" she asked, her small voice thickened by tears.

"Release you?" he murmured in genuine surprise, even as his body, mind, and soul protested the idea. "You are not a prisoner, Ana. You are my guest."

"Then I can go?"

Let her go? *Never*. "Alas, no."

"Why not?"

It was an excellent question; one she had every right to ask. He had been asking quite a few himself, in one form or another, for the past several weeks. They began with, 'What had happened the night of the after party?' and eventually became, 'What bond do I have with this woman?'. Now, with a single drop of her blood and an ardent wish to know the truth, he had answers to every one of those questions, and they were all centered upon one incontrovertible concept: Fate.

It was Fate that had brought this exquisite, rare creature quite literally to his doorstep. Fate that created this remarkable, rare bond between them.

And she had absolutely no idea.

Carefully schooling his features, he avoided that topic for the time being and focused on another, one no less true. "Because your very existence puts you in great danger beyond these walls."

"Are you telling me that I am in no danger here?" she sniffed, drawing out the words.

"Yes." He withdrew a fine linen handkerchief from his pocket and offered it to her. What he really wanted to do was press his lips to her skin and experience that crystal purity again.

She thought about that for a moment as she

dabbed at her eyes and her pert little pink nose. "But I wasn't in any danger out there either," she countered. "As long as no one knows." Her eyes widened. "You won't tell anyone, will you?"

His dormant heart thumped again as she stared at him with those big green eyes. Sympathy was not an emotion he felt often, but it washed over him in a substantial wave. She was far too innocent, far too trusting, if she thought a heartfelt plea would stop one of his kind from taking advantage of her. He was an exception, of course, but she had no way of knowing that. It only served to strengthen his belief that the safest place for her was with him.

"No," he answered honestly. "But without protection, it is only a matter of time before your secret is discovered."

"Matt protects me," she whispered.

Vlane's ire rose at the mention of the Alpha male's name from her lips. He set his mouth in a grim smile. "And yet, here we are."

Her lips parted as if to protest, but then closed again quickly. Her ability to see reason pleased him.

"What I find truly amazing," he told her, "is how you managed to stay undetected all this time."

"I'm not in the habit of sharing my… uniqueness," she explained quietly. "And I move around a lot." Her eyes brightened with hope. "If you let me go, I can leave town. I don't even have to go back to the Sanctuary…"

Her voice faded away when she saw him

shaking his head. "No, Ana. I cannot allow that. Someone will find you. There are those who would stop at nothing to have you." Vlane now fell into that category as well, but for entirely different reasons.

Her bottom lip trembled. "Why do you care what happens to me?"

He exhaled, knowing he could put it off no longer. Nothing but the truth would make her understand. "Because, Ana. You are my fated mate."

Her gasp was audible. "How—how can that be?" she asked, her eyes once again as wide as saucers. "Why would you say something like that?"

Vlane resumed his pacing. If he stared any longer into those beguiling green eyes, he would throw her beneath him and take what his body demanded. Even now, that tiny drop of blood upon his tongue made him desperate for more. With his thoughts in their current state of turmoil, he could not chance another "wish". Not until he knew he could control it — and her.

His best course was to attempt to explain things to her in a calm and rational manner, which was going to be difficult; he was still struggling to come to grips with it himself. When he and Armand had discussed the various possibilities, he dared not hope. Yet, now that he was with her, now that he had *tasted* her and knew the truth, there was no longer any doubt.

"You can hear my thoughts, yes?"

She nodded, a red tint rushing to her cheeks. No doubt she was remembering their last telepathic exchange and the dream that preceded it. It did absolutely nothing to help him focus.

"The only way that is possible is if some of my venom was unintentionally injected into you while I was feeding."

She blinked. At least she was no longer crying. Curiosity had crept into her gaze, temporarily pushing away some of the fear. "So? It was just a little bit, right?"

Annoyance flared within him. Why must she question him? Then he recalled the barrage of truths with which he'd been bombarded. His irritation was tempered by the knowledge that Ana was surprisingly naïve, and could not be expected to know such things.

"So," Vlane explained patiently, "a vampire's venom is only released in three circumstances, none of which are done commonly or lightly. All result in a permanent blood bond."

Ana inhaled sharply and wrapped her arms around herself again, as if that might shield her from what he was going to say next. Part of him wanted to snatch her up in his arms and hold her close, ease her fear with his kiss and touch. But another part — the part currently reeling from her nearness, from the scent of her skin and tears, doubted his ability to explain anything rationally with her warm body against his. And it was vitally important for her to understand.

"Two are done with the deliberate consent and intent of both parties. The first involves a ritualistic ceremony binding a human to a vampire until the human's life ends and its soul is released from its mortal shell. For all intents and purposes, it is a master-slave relationship. The human agrees to serve the vampire in return for care, protection, and feeding. Such bindings were more prevalent in the past, when survival was more difficult, though it has seen a resurgence in recent years with the popularization of vampire lore and the idealized romanticism of such a relationship. Obviously, that did not take place in our situation."

He paused, letting that sink in. "The second, of course, is when we sire another. That, too, is a conscious choice, for a human soul must willingly ask to be made vampire."

"A vampire can't turn another without permission?"

He frowned. "He can, but it is the greatest offense a vampire can commit. If discovered, he or she will be brought to trial. Unless extenuating circumstances dictate otherwise, the offender is sentenced to years of excruciating torture before being publicly and humiliatingly executed. But that is neither here nor there. You did not request to become vampire and I have made no attempt to turn you against your will."

"And what is the other circumstance?" she asked, her voice barely a whisper.

Vlane pinned her with his gaze. "When a vampire finds his true mate."

Ana sucked in a breath. Smiling wryly, he said, "Unlike the first two instances, the mating bond is one over which immortals — not just vampires — have no control. I did not even realize I had initiated the bond, but I did, when I sipped from you that night."

If he had known, he would not have wasted the last several weeks. After waiting half a millennium for a mate, he was more than ready. "When we are faced with the ones the Fates have decreed for us, the choice is taken out of our hands lest we squander it. It is the greatest of gifts."

"But… that night... how could you possibly have known that I was your…mate?"

"I didn't. Not until I tasted you. Even then, the memory of the encounter was hidden from me. I suspect that was a natural defense against my … indulgence. One intrinsic to your kind." It was brilliant, really. Anyone who unknowingly partook of such a creature's blood would not remember, thus greatly reducing the chance its secret would be revealed.

He ran his cool fingers over her cheek. "If I had remembered, I would not have waited so long to come for you."

"Maybe you're wrong," she offered hopefully.

"Maybe I'm not what you say."

"There is no doubt, Ana. The bond between us is irrefutable proof."

Ana looked rather pale, and she was trembling again, but she wasn't running. All of this had to be a shock to her, and as her mate, he needed to care for her. Now that he had explained things properly, there was no need to delay further.

"Come," he said suddenly, tugging her to her feet. He pulled her to his chest with one arm, lifting her as if she weighed nothing. His other hand cupped the back of her head and tucked it into his neck. He lifted his wrist to his mouth and allowed his fangs to lengthen. "You must drink my blood to seal the mating covenant."

She wrinkled her nose and pulled away. "Ew, no. I'm not doing *that*."

He looked at her as if she'd just sprouted horns. "Of course you are. As I have just explained, we are destined mates."

"Says you," she sniffed as she scrambled backward, bumping her legs and falling unceremoniously back onto the chair.

Despite his frustration, he almost grinned. Everything he'd told her had been absolutely true, but she had no way of knowing that. He would have to earn her trust. Beneath the meek and mild-mannered exterior, she was a clever girl.

But then, his mate would have to be.

Vlane decided to work with something a bit

more tangible, something she might have an easier time accepting. "You desire me. I know you do. I have seen your dreams."

Ana's delicate skin turned a deep shade of crimson as the blood rushed to her face. "So? Maybe I dream about other guys, too."

His face hardened. "There will be no other male for you. Ever. Only me. I am your mate."

Ana crossed her arms over her chest stubbornly and looked away.

Vlane gave her a lethal smile. "I can drink from you again and wish you to do the same," he said. "You do not have a prayer of stopping me, Ana."

All the color drained from her face, along with her momentary flare of courage as she met his gaze once again. "You...you would do that?"

He looked at her, at the way her eyes grew impossibly big and round, at the way her bottom lip trembled, and suddenly felt every bit the big, bad vampire he was. "I would prefer you choose to do so of your own accord," he said softly. "I am a patient man. I will do everything in my power to win your heart. But I can never let you go. It is not an option."

Against his baser instincts, Vlane turned on his heel and forced himself from the room, leaving her to assimilate that.

Chapter 15: Truth and Compromise

Vlane nudged the plate closer to her when the tender beef medallions, freshly herbed vegetables, and jasmine rice remained untouched. "Ana, please, eat something."

"I don't want to."

"I know you are hungry, Ana," he chastised, his voice soft. "I can sense it."

"I didn't say I wasn't hungry. I said I didn't want to eat."

Realization dawned. "Nothing was added to the meal. No harm will come to you by my hand."

She cast a doubtful look at him. He could hear her heartbeat, still a too-quick staccato, but less so than before. Despite being excessively gentle, she still feared him. In most cases, he reveled in such unease. But not now. Not hers.

"I wish you would."

She gave him a weak smile. "Is that a formal wish?"

He sighed deeply. "It is a heartfelt one."

She stared at him for a moment, then speared a carrot and brought it to her lips. He tracked the movement, but said nothing, watching as she followed with a bite of potato, a few beans, and a forkful of rice, leaving the meat untouched.

"You are vegetarian?" he guessed.

She nodded.

"My apologies," he said. "If I had been thinking clearly, I would have remembered the Fae were legendary for being in perfect harmony with the natural world. Taking the life of any sentient creature, for any reason, is probably abhorrent to you."

"It's okay," she sighed in resignation. "You already know more about my nature than I do."

Despite the power she held within her, she seemed so fragile, so delicate. Any previous suspicions he had of her using her unusual talents to weaken him faded quickly. This gentle creature, he was coming to believe, was incapable of harming anything. The Fates were either certifiably insane or beyond brilliant to place such a being in his hands.

"In my recent brief return to mortality, I found I am quite fond of peanut butter and jelly," he said thoughtfully.

Ana cast a surprised look his way, a gentle smile tugging at her mouth. The transformation was immediate. She went from simply beautiful to radiant, making him feel as though he was once again bathed in warm sunlight. And, fortunately for him, it was infinitely more pleasurable than actual sunlight.

"Peanut butter and jelly is good," she agreed,

spearing another carrot.

"Thank you," he said softly when she finished all of the vegetables and nibbled on a crusty roll.

"You're welcome. It *is* delicious, and I am hungry." She looked pointedly at the empty space in front of him. "Aren't you having anything?"

Vlane did something he hadn't done in a long time. He chuckled. "Are you offering, Ana?"

Ana flushed a becoming dark red hue and lowered her eyes. He found it as endearing as he did arousing.

"Come," he coaxed. Vlane led her to a warm and cozy sitting area. "Tell me about your magic."

Ana walked past the supple leather chair and settled herself into an oversized, upholstered one instead. Unwilling to put much distance between them, but not wanting to crowd her now that she seemed to be more at ease, Vlane chose the seat adjacent to hers.

"What do you want to know?" she asked.

Somewhat surprised by her easy acquiescence, he leaned back and asked, "Is blood necessary?"

It was a critical question. Throughout the ages, blood magic was the darkest and most powerful of all, often wielded beneath the guise of piety and innocence. From the précis Armand had given him, Fae magic was not historically blood-based, but every race had their secrets.

She focused her gaze on him. It was still wary, but she no longer seemed overly afraid of him. He took that as definite progress. Every minute he spent in her presence further convinced him she was his fated mate. Surely she must be feeling the rightness of it as well. If she could relinquish some of her fear, she might be able to recognize it. If only he could make her feel more comfortable…

"No. I can grant wishes at will, without blood."

"Would you show me?" he asked, fascinated.

Ana hesitated before nodding. She held out her hand, did a graceful twisting motion, then presented him with a black silk handkerchief embroidered with a cursive V and M.

"Extraordinary," he murmured, running the silk through his fingers. "And if I wanted something specific?"

"You could describe it to me, or I could simply touch you and get the sense of the wish directly."

Vlane held out his hand to her. She looked at it for several long moments before reaching out and letting her fingers brush lightly against his.

In the next moment, Samson was beside her, laying his big black and white head in her lap.

Ana looked questioningly at Vlane. His eyes widened almost imperceptibly. "I wished for something that would make you feel more at ease here." His lips tilted slightly. "I should have been more specific. Bast will not be pleased."

Ana's features softened. She stroked the big dog's head as he nuzzled her, obviously happy to see her again. Based on the look of gratitude on her face, Vlane decided it was worth it. Bast was clever and resourceful enough to hold her own.

"I'm still trying to figure it all out," she admitted. "But when someone takes my blood, he or she also takes my ability to control and censor the wish. The wish is granted in its purest form," she explained. "In your case, I think you became human because at that moment, it is what your heart desired above all else."

Vlane considered this. "And what if, in that moment, I desired the complete and utter destruction of the entire town?"

She didn't answer him, but she didn't have to. Darkness clouded her perfect eyes. Darkness did not belong on that beautiful face. "Hmm," he hummed beneath his breath.

They sat for long moments in silence until she asked, "Is that why you want me?"

"No, Ana," he said sincerely, hoping to ease her fears. "I have no intention of using you to vanquish my enemies, nor to obtain fame, wealth, or power. I have achieved all of those things on my own." He smiled slightly. "There is only one thing I desire now." He stared pointedly at her.

Her heartbeat quickened and he felt the instant rise in her body temperature. Yes, she understood exactly what he wanted. Her physical reaction told him she wanted the same thing, but she was fighting it.

"I will not grant that wish willingly," she

whispered.

He might have believed her, if he had not clearly heard the *yet* she had added silently to herself. Their mental connection was growing stronger with every passing minute.

He said nothing, continuing to stare at her, willing her to read his thoughts, to explore this miraculous bond they shared. He felt the tiniest brush, but she backed off almost immediately. It was disappointing, but as he had promised, he would be patient and earn her trust.

"Come. You must rest."

He waited, hand extended, until she slipped her much smaller hand into his. His dormant heart stuttered at the contact, jolted by the power flowing through him and the knowledge that she was coming willingly.

With Samson trailing closely behind, he led her to his bedroom. Stopping just inside the door, her gaze went immediately to the massive four-poster bed on a raised dais, covered in midnight blue satin.

"This is your guest room?" she asked doubtfully.

"No. You will stay with me," he told her, closing the door behind him.

"I don't think so."

He gave her an indulgent smile. Her weak attempts to refuse him had no real bite, yet they afforded her some measure of comfort as she grew to accept the idea that they belonged together. He would permit her to feel like she had some control, though they both knew it was a farce.

"It is the safest place for you. I am not the only vampire who lives on this estate. You have my word, I will not do anything you do not wish me to."

Ana sighed, but she did not protest further. At least she was being sensible.

"Do you wish me to draw a bath for you?"

"Can you do it in my house?" she said with a tiny, wry grin.

He smiled at the hint of teasing in her voice. He much preferred that to her fear. "Not tonight. Please, Ana, grant me this small boon?"

"It was worth a shot."

* * *

It was an effort to tear her eyes away from the massive bed approximately the size of her entire bedroom at the Sanctuary, especially when her mind's eye was creating all sorts of wholly inappropriate scenarios involving that dark blue satin and one sinfully gorgeous master vampire. Whether it was his influence or her own overactive imagination, she didn't know, but his feather-light touch along the small of her back was definitely not helping. It conjured images of other, more intimate caresses.

She might have gasped a little at one

particularly vivid mental picture. Vlane looked down at her from beneath hooded lids, his black eyes glistening and filled with desire. Did this supposed mental connection they shared allow him to sense her thoughts?

His lips quirked slightly, answering that question.

Ana forcibly wrenched her attention away from the bed to take in the rest of her immediate surroundings. Tasteful, hand-carved hardwood furniture enhanced the space. Soft, recessed lighting gave the room an intimate feel. The dark blue carpet was so thick, her feet sunk down several inches with each step. It was elegant and understated, yet decadent and extravagant.

Much like the man himself, she thought.

Vlane led her to the *en suite* bathroom. It was bigger than the studio apartment she'd had in veterinary school. The centerpiece was a sunken Jacuzzi tub, large enough to fit two comfortably. She watched as he ran the water, adjusting the temperature until satisfied. He opened no less than half a dozen brand new bottles of bath oils before he found one he liked. Then he methodically placed everything she could possibly want or need along the exquisitely tiled edge — soaps, creams, towels, exotic-looking sponges.

He draped a nightgown of pristine white silk beside the padded seat next to the tub, along with a matching silk robe and slippers.

"Have a lot of female guests, do you?" she asked, frowning at all of the feminine items he provided. A strange, unpleasant feeling rose up inside her at the thought. Though she'd never felt anything like it before, she recognized it as jealousy. And why, exactly, should she feel jealous over a man she barely knew?

Oh yes. Because they were fated *mates*.

"A vampire's lair is a very personal space. You are the first female to enter mine." For the first time, he looked a bit uncertain. "I have tried to anticipate your needs, but if you find anything lacking, please let me know and I will rectify the situation immediately."

A spark ignited somewhere deep in her chest. She searched his dark eyes for some indication he was lying, but found none. He had done all of this for her? The jealousy faded, replaced by gratitude. "Thank you, Vlane. That is very thoughtful of you."

"You are most welcome, Ana." He hesitated, as if he wanted to say more, but didn't. "I will leave you to your bath." With an old-fashioned bow, he left her alone with Samson.

The Newfie settled his big, furry body down in front of the door. He glanced up at Ana and panted softly. She understood his silent message: no one would be getting into the bathroom without going through him first.

"Thanks, Samson," she said softly. "I appreciate the effort."

Ana ran her fingertips over the smooth tile, wondering at the size of the tub. Yes, she wanted to go home, but surely a soak in what had to be the most decadent looking spa tub she'd ever seen would be okay, wouldn't it? And he had gone to all that trouble, which was really very sweet and thoughtful. It would be rude to refuse.

She undressed and slid into the scented water, unable to contain the groan of pleasure as she immersed herself in the hot water. After several minutes, she worked up the courage to turn on the twelve — twelve! — jets. Sinking back into the contoured seat, she let the pulsing water massage her from the bottoms of her feet all the way up to the base of her neck. She had never felt anything quite so deliciously indulgent before.

As her body relaxed, her thoughts naturally drifted toward her mysterious host and the unusual situation in which she now found herself. Was she now his prisoner?

No matter how much that might seem like the case, it didn't *feel* like that — not at all. Vlane was treating her as if she was an honored guest, providing chef-quality meals and luxurious accommodations. She felt more like a pampered guest.

And it wasn't as if he'd kidnapped her or forced her against her will. All it had taken was an invitation delivered in that smooth, rich, chocolate voice. Yes, they had some sort of telepathic connection, and she had felt the tug of his mild compulsion, but her will had remained her own. The need to comply with his request came from this inexplicable attraction she had to him. From a deep-seated desire strong enough to overcome her instinctual fear.

That was another thing — this strange bond between them. Vlane said it was because they were fated mates. Ana wasn't quite convinced of that just yet, but she did have to admit the man affected her unlike anyone else ever had. Sure, she had found men attractive before, but what she felt around Vlane Masterson went far beyond simple attraction or garden-variety lust. Unlike with Matt, it wasn't just her body that felt the pull, but her mind and heart as well. One look from those glittering, fathomless eyes stole her breath away.

The man had the most amazing eyes, she mused. Outwardly, his expression rarely changed (she would describe it as quietly stoic), but she was already beginning to figure out his moods, mostly through his eyes. She never knew there were so many different shades of black. They flared when he was angry. Sparkled when he was amused. And when they were deep, like crushed velvet, but not glittering, he was calm and curious.

But there was so much more to him than his perfect, masculine beauty and hypnotic eyes. When he spoke, she felt it in every cell of her body, like a caress. And his scent, dark, rich, and decadent, immediately calmed her. Ironically enough, she felt even safer in Vlane's lair than she had at the Sanctuary.

Could it be true, then? Could Fate or Destiny…or whatever controlled things, have determined the two of them belonged together?

It seemed impossible. Vlane was a master vampire and she…well, if Vlane was correct, she was one of the Fae. He was power personified and she was scared of her own shadow.

Yet, the very thought of him created a persistent tug upon her heartstrings, along with other, more embarrassing sensations. Beneath the water, her breasts swelled, her nipples hardened, and deep in her center, that persistent, slow-burning ache sparked into flame.

* * *

Ana? Vlane probed in her mind. He'd been pacing in his bedroom for nearly an hour, fighting the urge to go back to her. She called to him on such a visceral level. It was rather disturbing, really. Maybe it was part of her Fae magic, a spell of sorts she used, just as he could use his voice and will to compel.

Yesss, she answered back, her mental voice a sleepy drawl that had his cock swelling. Listening closely, he could hear that her heartbeat had slowed considerably.

Is everything all right? Is there anything you require?

Mmm, yes. A few more minutes in this heavenly tub, please. Her voice was a purr in his mind.

Surely the water must be cold by now.

I don't care.

Vlane smiled, feeling a small sense of triumph. He had found something that Ana liked about being here. Hopefully, there would be much more to follow.

Chapter 16: You Expect Me to Sleep Where?

It was an effort not to stare; she looked magnificent in the white silk gown. Like an angel.

"Where are you going to sleep?" she asked as he turned down the midnight blue duvet and pulled back the sheets so she could climb into the massive bed.

"I do not sleep," Vlane said matter-of-factly.

She blinked. "Never? How does that work?"

"I rest. It is more of a meditative state than actual slumber."

"Oh."

"Tonight, I will lay with you."

"Um..."

"It is for your safety, Ana." It was partially true. He could sense Kristoff prowling around the mansion, seeking the source of Ana's unique and enticing scent. Kristoff was loyal to him, but until he fully claimed Ana for himself, he would not take any unnecessary chances. But mostly, he just wanted to be near her, keep her in his sight.

"You have my assurance, I will do nothing more than watch over you. Are you warm enough? Shall I start a fire for you?"

"I'm fine. But there is something…"

He looked up and caught her staring at his arms and chest as he closed and latched the large windows. Hope surged through him when his acute senses picked up the quickening of her heart beat and the slight rise in her body temperature. Whether she wanted to admit it or not, she was attracted to him.

"Yes?"

She closed her eyes and shook her head, as if trying to dispel the image. He could have told her such a thing was futile. As mates, the desire would always be there. With every minute they spent in each other's presence, that desire would only grow stronger. Even with his remarkable self-control, he was having difficulty postponing the inevitable. It was only his desire to ease her transition that allowed such moral fortitude.

"Can I call my friend Dani, just to let her know I'm all right? She's probably worried."

He hesitated. He wanted to please her, but feared talking with her friend might undo some of the progress he had made. Yes, he and Matthew shared an uneasy truce, but there was no love lost between them, and neither side was foolish enough to blindly trust the other.

"Please," she said, touching his arm lightly

with her fingertips. "I have done everything you have asked."

He looked down and wondered how such a feather-light touch could infuse him with such warmth. Between that and the way she looked at him with those big, jewel-like eyes, he was swayed.

"All right," he agreed. It was a reasonable request, and chances were Matthew had already figured out where she was by using that exceptionally large nose of his. The last thing he needed was Matthew and his wolf pack descending upon his mansion before he convinced Ana she belonged with him.

* * *

"Dani? It's Ana."

"Ana! Oh my God! Where are you? Are you okay? You have us worried sick!"

Ana winced and pulled the phone away from her ear. Vlane was clearly listening from the far side of the room, but he wouldn't have needed his preternaturally acute hearing to hear the shrieks of the she-wolf.

"I'm fine, Dani. I just wanted to let you know that. Don't worry, okay?"

"Where are you? Matt, *back off*, I'm talking to her."

Matt apparently didn't listen, because it was his voice barking through the receiver next. "Ana?

Thank God. Did Masterson take you? I swear to God, if that bloodsucker hurts you, I'll rip his fucking throat out and piss in the hole."

Ana glanced at Vlane. His back was to her, but she saw him stiffen. "Matt, I'm fine. Really."

"Tell me where you are. I'll come get you. That leech can't hold you against your will—"

"No, Matt," Ana said, gently but firmly. Matt might be an Alpha, and he might be very powerful, but it would be suicide for him to attempt to try to force his way into Vlane's estate. Especially when she wasn't making any attempt to escape, and wasn't even sure she wanted to.

There was a long pause. "What do you mean 'no'?"

"I mean no. I'm okay. Samson's with me." Hearing his name, the Newfie woofed softly.

"Ana, listen to me. You might think you're safe, but you're not. Masterson and his ilk like to play with their prey. It's like some kind of sick game to them."

Ana bit her lip. She believed Vlane when he vowed he would not hurt her. Did that make her a fool?

In that moment, Vlane turned around and she met his eyes. His face was as stoic as ever, but his eyes…dear God, what she saw in them was nothing she ever expected to see in a five-hundred-year-old master vampire: Despair. Longing. Resignation.

"I'm fine," Ana insisted, infusing her voice

with the new sense of confidence building within her. She was safe here. And she wanted to learn more about this unusual bond she and Vlane seemed to share. "And you should know I came of my own volition. I was not forced."

"Bullshit!" Matt let loose a string of curses, making her wince again. "He's there, isn't he? He can hear everything you're saying, can't he?"

"Yes, he's here, but that doesn't change the truth," Ana said, wondering where her courage was coming from. "I'll call you tomorrow, okay? In the meantime, will you do something for me?"

"Christ, Ana," Matt exhaled heavily, "you know I would do anything for you."

She closed her eyes briefly, hearing the plea in his voice. She wanted to soothe his fears, but there was only so much she could do over the phone. "Watch over the Sanctuary until Sasha returns in a few days. If there are any emergencies, refer them down to Doc Carter in Bernsville."

"Ana—"

"Don't worry. I'm okay. Honest. Goodnight, Matt."

Ana disconnected the call before he could say anything else and set the phone on the nightstand. As she climbed between the sheets, a wave of exhaustion rolled over her. It had been a long, stressful day, but she was no longer afraid Vlane would hurt her. Had he wanted to cause her harm, he could have done so a dozen times over by now.

Samson leapt up on the bed and curled at her feet. She half-expected Vlane to say something about that, but he didn't. Instead, he walked over to the other side of the bed and lay down, fully dressed. They lay there like that in silence, side by side, her beneath the covers, him above, as the minutes ticked by.

"Why did you do that?" Vlane finally asked softly into the darkness. "Why did you defend me to the wolf when you know I compelled you? When I refuse to allow you to leave?"

Ana was kind of wondering that herself. It took several seconds for her to answer. "You might have compelled me to some extent, but no one can make me do something I don't want to. At least, not without taking my blood. So, on some level, I guess I wanted to come with you."

She let that sink in for a moment, realizing the truth of it even as she spoke. "I'd be lying if I said I haven't been kind of curious about you, too. And you have been nothing but kind to me since I got here, treating me like some kind of special guest."

"There is no one more special than you, Ana. Not to me."

She found it impossible to agree with that, but she was, by nature, a non-confrontational person. And very, very tired. "Vlane?"

"Yes?"

"Goodnight."

"Goodnight, Ana," he said softly, but she was

already asleep.

* * *

Vlane watched over her as her body and mind succumbed to the need for rest. Her features relaxed, making her look even younger, smaller. He couldn't remember the last time he had been in the presence of anything quite so fragile.

A quick mental prod ensured she was asleep. Unwilling to disturb her, he moved as close as he dared without actually touching her while the dog stared at him from the bottom of the bed. The warmth from her body seeped over into him and he soaked it in like a sponge.

They remained like that for a long time. Vlane was perfectly still, committing every facet of her features to memory. Then she turned in her slumber and snuggled up to him. Vlane had never felt such bliss. He closed his eyes, feeling a sense of peace wash over him.

Chapter 17: It's All Coming Back

"Fucking vampires." Matt was still muttering and cursing the next day. "He's manipulating her. Making her believe she's there by choice."

"Maybe she is," said Dani. Matt shot her a withering glare, but she ignored it. "Maybe she is where she wants to be. I mean, I know you think she's fragile and helpless and all, but she's not."

Matt glared at her. Ana *was* fragile. She was small, even by human standards. He could snap her in two with barely a thought, as could any member of his pack. Even Dani had to be careful when she gave Ana one of her exuberant hugs. He told her as much.

"Okay, she won't win any smack downs," Dani conceded, pointedly ignoring Matt's snarl. "But there aren't many who would win a physical contest against a vamp as old as Vlane Masterson. She's strong *inside*, Matt."

He laughed at that, but his wolf was so close to the surface, it came out sounding more like a bark. "Yes, she has spirit, but she's too soft. Christ, I've seen her stop her car in the middle of the road to move a frigging box turtle out of the way. And she's already proven she has little to no self-preservation instinct. She picked up a goddamn injured wolf from the side of the highway. What does that tell you?"

It was Dani's turn to glare. "Thank God she did. I wouldn't be here otherwise."

He sighed. "I know. I can't even think about what might have happened if she didn't."

And just that quickly, a slew of vivid, graphic images slammed into him. Memories he had somehow forgotten. Matt gripped the counter to retain his balance. It was as if a dam had suddenly given way and flooded his mind. "Son of a bitch."

"What's wrong?"

"That night…"

"What about that night?"

"Ana. She … did things."

"Yeah, she saved my life."

"No. I mean, yes, she did, but not like you think." At Dani's blank stare, he continued, "You were too out of it. You didn't see her that night. I did."

That gave Dani pause. "What are you talking about?"

"She helped you, Dani, but you almost killed her."

"What?" Dani suddenly felt ill. The color drained from her face and she leaned back against the sofa. "I would never hurt Ana."

"You were out of your mind, Dani. You didn't know what you were doing."

"Tell me."

Matt looked as though he'd rather do anything but. He closed his eyes against the images of that night. Of his baby sister lying on the table, broken and bloodied, barely clinging to life. Of the tiny human (or so he thought) female nearly looking as bad, working frantically over her. He could even hear Ana's words in his head as she repeated them, over and over: *Want to live! Want to heal! Wish it!*

It hadn't made sense then, but it did now. Dani had tasted Ana's blood; she must have in the many times she'd ripped into her flesh. "She let you bite her because she knew it was the only way to save you."

The onslaught of images continued, each one more horrific than the last. How could he possibly have forgotten?

"Matt, what are you talking about? That doesn't make any sense."

"Dani, there's something you need to know about Ana…"

"Why didn't you tell me?" Dani whispered after Matt explained it all to her.

Matt didn't have a suitable answer. Even now, he felt Ana's bloodied hand on his chest, over his heart, speaking to him in that soft voice, making him forget.

"She…asked me not to. She knew you would

feel bad about it. I didn't understand. I didn't know about her blood then, what it could do. I thought she was just a crazy human with a death wish, but the next time I saw her, her injuries were just minor, so I thought I'd imagined it. Christ, Dani, you're my baby sister, and you were in such bad shape. It was all so hazy…"

* * *

Dani sank back into the sofa and closed her eyes, trying to shut out the gory images Matt's explicit descriptions crafted. She could almost see it. Sasha screaming for help. Ana trying to break the grip of Dani's jaws from her arm. Ana straddling over her in an attempt to keep her still enough to shoot her up with some tranquilizers. Ana pleading with her to want to pull through. And finally, the look of shock on Ana's face when Dani whipped her head up in one final lunge and clamped it around Ana's neck…

That she could do such things to Ana revolted and horrified her. Matt was right. Ana was tiny. She was fragile. By all logic, she never should have survived.

She never should have survived…

"Matt," Dani said slowly, her voice shaky as her own vivid memories returned in a rush. "I tore out her throat."

Matt shook his head. "No. She was in bad

shape, but not that bad."

Dani knew better. She *remembered*. Suddenly, a flood of other memories resurfaced, too. Of Ana cradling her to her neck, telling her it would all be okay. Of sitting in Ana's kitchen only a few days ago while Ana told her about her blood and what it could do.

"She messed with our memories," Dani said, feeling the truth of it. Her big, golden brown eyes met Matt's. "She didn't want us to know."

"Didn't want us to know what?"

"*She's immortal.*"

* * *

When Ana's rumbling stomach woke her, she was alone, but something told her she hadn't been so for long. Though she had been sleeping solo her entire life, she now felt strangely bereft. Rolling over, the sheets were cool, but that wasn't enough to suggest how long ago he'd left. Vlane's skin was not as warm as a human's, and definitely did not hold the heat of a Were. It wasn't unpleasant, though.

The pillow next to hers held his scent. She buried her face in it and breathed in deeply; it reminded her of moonlight and the first cool nights of autumn.

With a stretch, she sat up, feeling more rested than she had in weeks. A rhythmic thumping drew her gaze to the floor, where Samson sat beside a large ceramic bowl of water and an empty food dish.

Her heart swelled. *Vlane had taken care of Samson while she slept in.*

Ana swung her legs over the side of the bed and slid to the floor. After greeting Samson with a few words and a nice scratch, she padded into the massive bathroom to see to some necessities. When she was finished, she searched for something to wear. The scrubs she had arrived in were nowhere to be found and the sexy, white, silk lingerie left her feeling a little too exposed to go wandering about the mansion in search of something to eat.

The massive walk-in closet was a study in black: black slacks, black jeans, black shirts, black shoes. Why was she not surprised? The man was a study in black. She wondered if he really liked the color that much or if it was some kind of vampire thing, symbolic and fitting for so-called 'creatures of the night'. Clearly, Vlane was able to move and function during the daylight hours. She would have to ask him about that at some point.

There was so much she didn't know about immortals. About vampires. About Vlane. What she did know is that at some point over the last twenty-four hours, things had changed dramatically. Nearly all of her fear had vanished, and in its place was an underlying feeling of contentment. Of rightness. As if, after years and years of moving around, she was finally exactly where she belonged.

Could it be true? Had everything brought her here, to this time, this place, this…possible mate?

It seemed impossible, and yet, not. Ana was no longer in any hurry to leave. The situation – and Vlane – definitely warranted further study.

Ana selected one of the many identical black silk shirts, then slipped it over her head. It hung down past her knees, but felt cool and smooth, and smelled like Vlane.

She held up a pair of pants, shaking her head. Vlane had a foot on her at the very least, but beggars couldn't be choosers, she supposed. She located a belt (black, of course) and cinched the slacks around her waist the best she could before proceeding to roll up the cuffs several times until she was able to take a step without tripping.

She emerged from the closet to find Vlane standing in the bedroom, looking for her, holding a tray with coffee, juice, muffins, and luscious-looking fruit-filled crepes.

At the sight of Ana in his clothes, he stilled. She felt the intensity of his gaze all the way down to her bare toes.

"I'm sorry," she told him apologetically. "I didn't have anything else to wear."

* * *

Vlane set the tray down with great care,

stretching every last thread of control he possessed to its limit. Even as ridiculously dressed as she was, she was the most beguiling woman he had ever met. Her golden hair tumbled down past her hips in cascading, riotous waves. Her green eyes, so filled with innocence and inquisitiveness, sliced through his cynical nature like lasers. And her lips were full and so perfectly pink, matching the pearlescent shade on the tiny toes peeking out from beneath the cuffs of his black slacks.

There was not a cell in his body that did not wish to claim her — fully and completely — in that moment. To enter her body as she entered his.

But it was not simply her beauty that called to him. It was her gentle heart. Her sweetness. Her naïveté. She *did* things to him, beyond keeping him in a near-constant state of arousal. Ana revived feelings in him that he thought had been lost forever. Hope. Light. *Love*.

Yes, he realized. He loved her.

It was a shocking thought, even believing as he did that she was meant to be his. They knew so little of one another, and yet he knew that his feelings for her ran far deeper than any he had ever felt for another. Perhaps that was part of the gift, the grain of truth beneath the romanticized ideal of love at first sight, given to fated mates upon finding one another.

A heartbeat later, she was in his arms, the hard length of his body pressed against her softer, fuller curves. "You are mine, Ana," he said, heat and passion firing in his blood. Fate had brought her to him. She was a precious gift, crafted for him and him alone.

Vlane nuzzled her neck, his fangs extending in anticipation, just as his cock filled and lengthened, both wanting desperately to be inside her. One taking, the other giving, creating a circle that would bind them irrevocably. Ana offered no resistance. It wouldn't have mattered if she had; resistance was futile against a vampire in full-blown bloodlust.

Eventually, it was her compliance that gave him pause. In his lust, he hadn't used an ounce of compulsion. "You do not fight me," he murmured against the pounding tempo of her pulse. "Do you want this?"

"Yes," she whispered. "I do want you."

It was quite possibly the only thing she could have said that would have allowed him to stop. *Ana wanted him.* And because she did, he would court her, seduce her properly, until she not only wanted him, but could not breathe without him. He stilled, letting her heat and scent soak into him. He used it to find the strength to release her.

Looking in her eyes, he expected to see triumph, or at the very least, relief, but he found neither. What he saw was infinitely more powerful. No one had ever looked at him so...*possessively.* As if he was the one who belonged to her. And in that moment, Vlane Masterson realized that for the first time in nearly five hundred years, he was at the mercy of another.

She knew it, too. Vlane probably should have despaired, but it was impossible to do so when she looked at him with a want so pure in nature, it nearly burned him. In a tender move, she touched her fingertips to his chest, right above his quiet heart.

I will never hurt you.

The words resounded in his head and echoed through his entire body.

He couldn't help but wonder why she would say such a thing to him and in such an intimate manner. Then, he realized she was touching him and had heard his heart's deepest desire: that she, now his greatest weakness, would not destroy him, but love him in return.

I will never hurt you.

The words replayed in his heart and mind, again and again. On the heels of those followed the knowledge that Ana was incapable of lying. He closed his eyes and savored the feeling of peace and joy they brought to him. It wasn't exactly a declaration of love, but it was enough.

For now.

He gathered her in his arms once again, more tenderly this time. He stroked the golden silk of her hair, soaking up the warmth of this exquisite creature who had somehow managed to slay him with nothing but a few words that reached the depths of his soul.

"Do you now believe me, Ana? That you are my fated mate?"

She sighed against his chest. "I'm not completely convinced of that. But I do know I have never felt for anyone the way I feel for you. You have to be patient with me, Vlane. This is not an easy thing to accept."

Her words filled him with hope. "That is all right. I will spend the rest of my life convincing you, though I sincerely hope it does not take that long."

Ana laughed softly. He could feel the warm puffs of air through his shirt as he loosened his hold. "Come now. I have brought you breakfast."

"You are an incredibly sweet man," she murmured, beaming at him. Had anyone else dared to call him that, he would have shown them exactly how untrue that statement was. But when Ana said it, he could do nothing more than blink at her.

She grinned. "Thank you for breakfast. It smells wonderful."

Her attempt to distance herself from him snapped him back to the present. Fisting his hands by his side to keep from pulling her right back into him, he watched her lean over the tray and inhale deeply. "Mmm, peaches. My favorite."

The corners of his lips quirked as he watched her. She looked absolutely ridiculous in his clothes. Ridiculous and incredibly adorable, yet there was one thing puzzling him. "Tell me, sweet Ana, why you simply do not call forth clothes of your own?"

The shy way she looked up at him would be etched in his memory forever. "I can't."

"But you are Fae. You have the ability to grant wishes."

"I can only grant the wishes of others," she said, her cheeks coloring in embarrassment. "Not my own, unless it is a wholly selfless wish."

Vlane was staggered by the thought. How cruel were the Fates to bestow such power upon one who could not use it for herself? It did, however, explain why she would be working as a human, living in the modest accommodations provided by others instead of some grand mansion. Though, he didn't think Ana would do that even if she could.

He ran his thumb over her cheek. "Then I will be the one who sees that your wishes are granted," he said softly. "What is your preference? You have only to name it, and it shall be yours."

She looked down at herself, smoothing the front of the shirt. "A pair of jeans would be nice."

He blinked, something he rarely did. Jeans and his shirt? When she could have *anything*? Clearly she did not comprehend the true depth of what he was offering — the finest silks, furs, jewels, gowns. But when he said as much, she shook her head and smiled shyly at him. "I like your shirt. It's comfortable and it smells like you."

How could he possibly argue with that?

Chapter 18: On Pixies and Fairies and Battles

"She looks like Tinkerbell," Kristoff remarked, shaking his head in wonder. He stood in Vlane's office, watching Ana on the security camera. Vlane had given her the freedom to explore his expansive mansion, but requested she not go outside. It was a test, of sorts, to see if she would attempt to flee. If she did, he would know the spell she had cast on him earlier had been nothing but a magick trick, but he highly doubted it. The hold she had on him was an entirely different kind of magick, one over which no one – immortal or otherwise – had any control.

"Like who?" Vlane asked. So far, Ana had given no indication she would try to escape. She couldn't, of course. Jason and Zarek were never far away from her, and the guard around the house and perimeter had been doubled. For the last hour, she had been in the library, running her hands over the leather bound volumes, occasionally picking up a tome and paging through it with nothing less than reverence on her face.

The dog, as usual, was with her. It had

appointed itself her protector, remaining close to her side as she moved through the hundred room mansion. Under normal circumstances, that would have annoyed him, but the hairy creature was obviously a source of comfort to her. And, if he was honest, the canine afforded him a bit of comfort as well. The few times one of his household had neared the room, Samson had moved in close to Ana and gone on full alert. Odd, though, how it seemed to have accepted *him* easily enough. Even odder that he found himself warming up to the beast. That morning he'd felt compelled to ensure the dog had food and water while it stood guard over Ana.

Kristoff shot him an irritated look. "*Tinkerbell.* You really need to join the twenty-first century, Vlane."

At Vlane's blank expression, he continued. "Tinkerbell is an animated creation of the human Walt Disney. A *faerie*," he said, with particular emphasis. When that also failed to elicit any recognition, Kristoff conjured up an image for him. Like a 3D hologram, it rotated slowly in the air before them.

Vlane's eyes widened as he took in the big, jeweled green eyes, slightly angled. The mischievous innocence of her expression. The sunshine-blonde hair falling haphazardly over her forehead. As the figure turned, he also recognized the lush breasts, tiny waist, and shapely behind.

"Actually, Tinkerbell is a pixie, not a faerie." Armand's voice suddenly cut in as he joined them.

"What's the difference?" Kristoff asked.

"Pixies are notoriously devious," he answered without hesitation. "Ana is no pixie."

Vlane tore his eyes away from Kristoff's image to look at Armand, but the other vamp had his eyes pinned to the real Ana on the screen. "I have never seen a soul as pure as hers," Armand continued almost absently. He looked at Vlane pointedly. "She is an innocent, in body as well as spirit."

Armand, a scholar and priest in his former life, had been gifted with seeing inside a person's soul upon his conversion. Vlane often wondered what Armand saw when he looked at his soul, though he'd never asked.

"She's got a great ass," Kristoff noted.

Vlane growled deep in his throat, allowing his substantial power to fill the room, his message clear. Ana was his.

Kristoff wisely dropped his eyes. It was the closest he would come to offering an apology. Vlane accepted it for what it was and turned his focus back to Armand. "Speak that which is on your mind, old friend."

Armand took a deep breath, something wholly unnecessary since they had no need to breathe. Sometimes, though, old habits resurfaced, even after hundreds of years. "She can destroy you."

Kristoff shifted uncomfortably as Vlane

stiffened. "No harm will come to me by her hand," he said, repeating the sentiment she had shared with him earlier, his voice deep and laced with conviction.

Armand studied him carefully. After several long moments, he exhaled and placed his hand on Vlane's shoulder. "For all of our sakes, but especially yours, my friend, I hope you are right."

Any further discussion halted as they all received an urgent mental prod from Jason. "Sire, the western perimeter has been breached."

The three vampires turned their attention to the screens. Kristoff pressed a few keys, switching the screens to display the images from the security cameras they had posted along those boundaries. Vlane's lip curled when he caught a flash of golden-colored fur.

"It is Matthew," Armand said quietly. "He has come for Ana."

"He will be disappointed," Vlane snarled. There was no way he would willingly relinquish Ana now — not to the wolf or anyone else. He flashed to the library with all haste. He would ensure Ana was well protected, then he would deal with the wolf Alpha personally and end this once and for all.

Vlane stood in the middle of the cavernous room, turning in a full circle before reaching out with his senses to learn that which his eyes had already told him: Ana was gone.

Vlane, come. Had his heart actually been beating, it would have stopped entirely at Kristoff's terse command. When Vlane returned to the office only a few seconds after he left it, he followed Kristoff's gaze to the screens.

Ana was running toward the western boundary, Samson at her heels.

As far as battles went, it was incredibly short-lived. Unlike the movies, real deadly predators did not face off over long, tense moments, giving and taking punishment in spectacular but essentially harmless moves. Disabling blows were delivered swiftly and decisively by both sides, often only a single strike necessary to fell an opponent.

By the time Vlane arrived, the downed warriors of both sides were strewn across the west lawn, werewolves and vampires alike. Zarek was badly wounded, but Jason was already giving him the blood he needed to heal. Other vamps were being tended to in a similar manner.

Vlane searched frantically for Ana, finding her kneeling in the grass beside the fallen Alpha.

* * *

Derrick, bloodied and battered, hunched over Matt's still form. He looked at Ana, begged her to do something. Ana knew it was all her fault. She cradled Matt's head in her lap while she used her special skills to assess his injuries. It didn't take long for her to determine Matt would die if she didn't do something soon.

Get away from him, Ana, Vlane commanded.

Ana looked at him, her face wet with tears. *I must save him.* She allowed her thoughts to flow into his, strong on the waves of her emotion.

If you give him your blood, I will lose you forever.

Ana looked down, her tears falling on Matt's face, cutting through his blood like diamonds in a red river. She met Derrick's eyes, saw his desperate plea there. Those few seconds lasted an eternity, but Ana knew what she had to do. She shared her thoughts with Vlane, who looked uncertain, but nodded.

Vlane flashed out of sight as she brought her wrist up to her mouth and tore into her own flesh. But instead of pouring her blood over Matt's wounds, she thrust her wrist in Derrick's face. Derrick turned his head in horrified disgust, but Vlane appeared behind him. He held the adolescent Were easily with one arm, using the other to pry open Derrick's jaw.

Ana sealed the opening with her wrist and pinched Derrick's nose shut, forcing him to swallow or risk suffocation. He struggled for a moment before his eyes grew heavy with unwanted pleasure.

No longer fighting, he grabbed Ana and pulled her closer. After several strong pulls, his body went lax. Vlane released him and scooped Ana into his arms.

* * *

Matthew woke, feeling groggy and sore. It took him a few minutes to realize he was in Ana's room back at the Sanctuary. An immense sense of relief filled him when he saw Ana speaking quietly with Derrick. Surprisingly, Derrick didn't even look his way. Ana went up on her tiptoes and kissed Derrick on the cheek, stroking his hair fondly. With a goofy, awkward smile, Derrick left with stars in his eyes.

Matt knew instantly what she had done. "You made him forget."

Ana turned at the sound of his voice, offering him a sad smile. "Not everything, but some, yes."

"Will you make me forget, too, Ana?"

Ana came and sat beside him, taking his much larger hand in hers. "Do you want me to?" she asked softly.

Matt closed his eyes, knowing, in that moment, he had already lost her.

"It wasn't meant to be, Matt," she told him, stroking his hair back from his face. Her touch was so gentle, so loving. It hurt like hell.

"I would be a good mate for you, Ana."

She smiled. "Yes, you would," she agreed. "But I would not have been a good mate for you."

Matt opened his mouth to disagree, but the pads of her fingers touched his lips lightly. "You know it is true, Matt. You need a woman worthy of an Alpha. A woman strong of body and heart who can give you what you need. With me, you would always know fear. Fear of what others might do to me if they learned my secrets. Fear of what you might do in a moment of passion."

"I can change you."

"You could, but then I would lose who I am, and I'm not willing to do that."

Matt's throat constricted, knowing she was right. But she had to know. He had to say the words at least once. "I love you, Ana."

Her eyes softened, yet still glittered like fine, pale gems. "I love you, too, Matt, and I always will. No matter what, I will always be here for you, and your pack. But one day, your true mate will come along, and make what you feel for me pale in comparison. She is out there, Matt. I know she is."

He nodded and Ana leaned over, kissing his eyes, his nose, then his mouth, murmuring softly in a language he did not understand. It sounded like beautiful music, wrapping around his heart and filling him with a sense of profound peace and light and love as he drifted back into a healing sleep.

* * *

"Are you all right?" Vlane asked, taking Ana's

elbow as they walked down the cobbled walkway to where his car awaited them.

"I will be," she said with a brave smile.

Leaving those she cared for with little or no memory of her was always hard, yet she took some comfort in the fact that it made it easier on them. Most of those involved in the attack had been healed; those few who could not be saved through normal means were given the option of becoming vampire. Vlane and his brood assisted in altering the memories of the pack, which had helped tremendously.

Vlane opened the car door for her and saw her in, then rounded to the driver's side and slid behind the wheel. "What now?"

She touched his arm and his heart filled with light. "Now, we go home."

Chapter 19: Don't Mess With Destiny

"It was brilliant, giving your blood to Derrick like that," Vlane said as he slipped off his black leather shoes inside his private suite and loosened the topmost buttons of his shirt.

"I knew he would wish for Matt to make a full recovery." She smirked. "I have been doing this a while, you know."

Vlane stalked silently over to Ana. Grabbing the hem of her shirt, he lifted it over her head, sucking a breath through his teeth when he saw the sexy black lace covering her lush breasts.

He swore in an ancient, beautiful language and fell to his knees before her. His fingers traced the lace as he undid the button on her jeans and began to peel them from her body. Ana had chosen him. Willingly. And he wasn't wasting a moment more.

"Do you know what my most heartfelt wish is in this moment?" he asked, his voice barely audible as he pressed reverent kisses to her tender flesh. Her fingers curled into his hair, releasing it from its leather tie to fall in shiny, black silk waves around his face.

"No."

"It is to pleasure you, Ana. Will you grant my wish?"

She said nothing, but snaked her arms around his neck in silent affirmation. He lifted her effortlessly onto the bed and positioned himself over her, then pressed her back against the pillows and began to kiss her. She became lost in the feel of his tongue on her body, his hands kneading and caressing with the expertise of a man who had been pleasuring women for half a millennium.

He worked his way down her body. Gently, but firmly, opened her to him. Kissed her where no man had ever touched her before. Her hands clutched at his hair as a tidal wave of sensations crashed over her, pulled her under, then did it all again. And again. Cresting higher each time until she begged him for mercy.

When he finally gave her that blessed release, she screamed his name.

* * *

Vlane had never heard anything sweeter. He did it twice more before she fell into an exhausted, but satisfied slumber.

He watched her sleep. It had been a traumatic time for her and his attentions drained the last of the fight out of her. That was all right with him. He would gladly devote the rest of his life to such matters if it would keep her in his bed, screaming his name.

He licked his lips, tasting her. The sweet nectar she had spilled for him was every bit as rich and decadent as her blood. Of course, he wanted that, too.

She was an innocent. Untouched by any man. He would be her first. Her last. Her only. The knowledge filled him with more satisfaction than his eternal youth, superior power, and ungodly wealth combined.

His *mate*.

The idea still boggled his mind. He hadn't exactly been alone the last five hundred years; his progenies were his family, and their blood bonds were as strong as, if not stronger than, those of a traditional human family. But the relationship between a man and his mate was something else entirely. Having a true mate, one fashioned by the Fates, meant that they would share their lives with a level of intimacy beyond compare. Forevermore, this amazing woman, this beautiful Faerie, would be by his side. The other half of his soul.

* * *

Her dreams were even more realistic than usual. This time, she knew the skill of those fingers, the things he could do with that mouth, the erotic scrape of his fangs along the most feminine parts of her — teasing, warning, *possessing*. But as wonderful as those things were, she needed more.

Vlane slipped into her thoughts, into her dreams where she began to grow increasingly unsettled. Through their special connection, he had heard her soulful plea.

He slid over the top of her body, the heavy weight of him betwixt her thighs. He groaned when he slid his fingers along the wet, swollen flesh of her sex.

"Ana," he murmured. "Wake up. Wake up and let me grant your most heartfelt wish."

She opened her eyes as her dream slid into reality. Vlane was on top of her here, too. His hard body weighed solidly on hers; black eyes glittered with a fierce hunger and a desire to please. He held himself, poised at her entrance, yet he did not force himself upon her as he so easily could have.

"Say yes. Say yes and I will ease that unbearable ache inside you. Want this, Ana. Want *me*."

In that moment, Ana knew there was absolutely nothing she wanted more than to join with him fully, and it was purely her own thought. She'd felt what it was like to have him inside of her mind. Already knew his intimate kiss on the most feminine part of her. Now, she felt achingly empty — and she didn't like it.

"Yes." She drew out the word, a long, slow

hiss.

His black eyes flashed with triumph. He rolled his hips forward and penetrated her, piercing through her innocence even as his fangs pierced her neck. He grew thicker, harder inside of her with each pull of her blood into him, and she knew what he wanted more than anything else: to please her.

And, like the powerful faerie she was, his wish was granted. Tenfold.

Vlane took her all night. Loved her. Possessed her in every possible way, fulfilling her every fantasy, over and over again. As each new desire took form, he was there in her mind, growling with approval, turning it into reality.

By the time he thrust deep and emptied inside her, again, she was well past coherent thought. There was only Vlane. He was inside her, and she in him. No longer two separate souls, but one.

And nothing had ever felt so right.

* * *

"Do you not worry what wish may cross my mind as I take your blood into me?" Vlane asked, nuzzling the delicate skin along her neck. He would never again know the taste of another; there was only his Ana. She alone would sustain him, as he would sustain her. Forever.

"No, not anymore."

He propped himself up on his elbows and

looked down at her. "Why not?"

She smirked at him. "You don't know?"

He shook his head, bemused.

"Because we are now one."

He still looked confused, so she took pity on him. "And the two shall become one? In the case of true soul mates, that's *really* true."

Vlane blinked. "So, I'm a faerie now?"

She laughed. "In a manner of speaking, yes. My blood now runs through your veins, which means you can no longer wish anything for yourself, only others."

She allowed that to sink in, playing with his hair while he processed that. She knew he was testing her theory, trying to wish for something, anything. He smiled when he realized she was right.

"Does it stand to reason, then, if you took some of my blood you would become vampire?"

Ana grinned, showing him the tiny fangs now gracing the upper tier of her teeth where her regular incisors had been. "Yes."

"When did you—?"

Ana blushed furiously and shuttered her eyes. "I got a little carried away when you made me climax that seventh time."

A smile of pure male arrogance lit his features as he remembered the way she had screamed, how her nails had scored his back, how her teeth had clamped onto his shoulder as she seized with ecstasy.

"So you did." He nuzzled her again, taking the opportunity to slide into her.

"Ana," he breathed, his strokes long and thorough.

"Hmm?"

"Would you do me the honor of becoming Mrs. Vlane Masterson?"

"You picked a heck of a time to propose. How can I possibly say no when you're...doing...*that*?" Ana forced the last few words out as Vlane did something particularly wicked with a twist and thrust of those talented hips.

"You're not supposed to say no," he said, nipping beneath her jaw.

"Are all vampires as devious and arrogant as you?"

"No. I am by far the most devious and arrogant of all vampires."

Ana laughed, flexing her sheath possessively around him. "In that case, I would be honored to be your wife, Mr. Masterson."

Chapter 20: HEA in 3, 2, 1...

The entire town of Mythic was invited to witness the vows between one of its most prestigious citizens and his beloved during an elegant twilight service.

Matthew sat with his youngest sister and the rest of his pack.

"Do you know the bride?" Dani whispered, her brow furrowing slightly as she watched the small figure escorted up the red-velvet runner between the chairs. "She looks awfully familiar."

He had been thinking the same thing, but he couldn't remember where he might have seen her before. Surely, he would remember a woman as beautiful as Vlane's bride.

Later, during the reception, he would find himself wondering again when he took his turn during the traditional bridal dance. Something sad and poignant flashed in the bride's eyes as he held her.

"Do I know you?" he blurted out before he could stop himself.

"My name is Ana," she said, her voice soft and musical. "I'm a vet. Sasha lets me help out at the Sanctuary on Tuesdays and Thursdays."

"Oh. That must be where I've seen you. Thanks. For helping out, I mean."

She flashed him another smile tinged with what could only be described as sadness before he was touched on the shoulder by another guest wishing to dance with the bride. As he released her, he heard a ghostly echo in his head, like some long ago memory. *I will always be here for you.*

Matt shook his head. Clearly, he'd partaken a little too heavily of the open bar.

"Matthew," said a deep voice, "thank you for coming and sharing this day with us."

Matt turned around to find Vlane Masterson. Funny how just a few months ago he could have sworn Masterson hated him and his pack with a vengeance, but he couldn't have said why. Tonight, however, there was no hint of hostility between the Weres and the vamps. Vlane and his people — for lack of a better word — had been nothing but gracious and excellent hosts.

"Thanks for inviting us."

* * *

Vlane nodded. Ana laughed at something Karthik, the demon lord said, playfully swatting his arm. *Only Ana could get away with doing*

something like that to the vicious demon, Vlane
thought. Then again, he had yet to come across a
male of any species who was immune to his bride's
Fae charms.

"You are a better male than I, vampire," Matt
said, watching the scene. "If I were in your place, I
don't know that I'd let my female dance with the
likes of him. Or you, for that matter."

Vlane laughed. "If you were in my place, wolf,
you would know my bride can take care of herself,
as well as the true peace that comes with finding the
other half of your soul."

At that moment, Ana turned and spied Vlane.
Her entire face lit up at the sight of him. As Armand
grabbed her and spun her around to dance, Vlane
turned back to Matt. "It is truly a gift I wish for all
men."

Vlane left Matt when Derrick and a few others
headed in their direction.

"Did you really mean that?" Ana said,
surprising him by coming up beside him and
wrapping her arms around his waist.

"Mean what?" he asked, leaning down to place
a kiss on her lips. Chaste as it was, Vlane
embellished it with promises of what was to come
the moment they were alone. It couldn't come soon
enough for him, but he reminded himself that they
had an eternity in front of them. It was a happy
thought.

"That you wish every other male here would

find their soul mate?"

"How did you—?"

She grinned. "Vampire hearing, remember? Compliments of my husband — the biggest, baddest vampire of them all."

He laughed and pulled her tightly against him. "Yes, my love. I did mean it. Why?"

"Because," she said, her eyes twinkling mischievously, "we can make that happen…"

Thanks for reading Vlane and Ana's story

If you liked this book, then please consider posting a review online! It's really easy, only takes a few minutes, and makes a huge difference to independent authors who don't have the mega-budgets of the big-time publishers behind them.

Log on to Amazon (or Goodreads) and just tell others what you thought, even if it's just a line or two. That's it! A good review is one of the nicest things you can do for any author.

As always, I welcome feedback. Email me at abbiezandersromance@gmail.com. Or sign up for my mailing list on my website at http://www.abbiezandersromance.com for up to date info and advance notices on new releases, Like my FB page (AbbieZandersRomance), and/or follow me on Twitter (@AbbieZanders), Instagram, Pinterest, GooglePlus, and soon, Tumblr.

Thanks again, and may all of your ever-afters be happy ones!

 Abbie

If you liked this book...

... then check out this excerpt from the next book in the Mythic Series, *Fallen Angel*...

Scrubbed clean and dressed in acceptable human attire, Ryssa worked her way through the woods that separated the bad part of town from the good on tired, aching feet. Wealth was not necessarily a good thing, in her opinion. Oh, there were benefits, of course, she thought as she took in the huge, imposing manor house. Money could get you a warm, dry place to live. It could pay for good food and cover your back with some nice clothes. Help others in need, if you were the charitable sort. But this place was more than meeting basic needs. This place was over the top.

You couldn't even call it a house, not by any stretch of the imagination. A mansion, maybe. Small castle, more like. How many people actually lived here? The place was bigger than three of the run-down tenement buildings she called home put together. And what was *that* behind the manicured topiaries? A freaking tennis court?

She winced as a bright motion-sensor floodlight blazed in her face. What the hell was it with people and these damn floodlights these days? If God had intended light to be a twenty-four hour thing, he wouldn't have bothered with the moon and the stars.

It forced her to focus, though. She'd been so busy gap-jawing at the sheer size of the place that she hadn't been paying much attention. Good thing they were just floodlights and not bloodthirsty Dobermans or she'd be dog food by now. She might not be able to die, but she could hurt a hell of a lot in the time it took to heal.

Taking a deep breath, she rang the doorbell. From far away, soft chimes sounded the notes of some classical masterpiece. Bach, she thought idly, going back to an eon ago and a universe away. Now there was a guy who knew how to party, she thought with a quirk to her lips.

It was the middle of the night. Whoever behind the door was probably long since in bed and wouldn't be happy to be disturbed, but it was what it was. They summoned her, not the other way around. They would have to work with her timeline. Besides, a place this big probably had a slew of servants around the clock who got paid to answer the door at all kinds of ungodly hours.

Ryssa was forced to adjust that preconceived notion a moment later. The guy who opened the door was no servant.

The scent of expensive men's soap hit her first. She looked at the wall of the muscled male chest in front of her, tightly wrapped in a high-quality designer shirt. A shiver ran down the length of her spine.

Lifting her gaze, she found cold green eyes looking down on her with absolute derision. Those eyes travelled down the length of her petite body over the span of several heartbeats, taking in her threadbare jeans, ratty sneakers, and plain black cotton T.

"No solicitors."

The man's upper lip actually curled when he said it. Without the snarl, she might have considered him handsome. His features were classically male and well-proportioned. Dark auburn hair cut close at the nape, and deep, penetrating green eyes that might have sparkled under different circumstances.

Ryssa stuck her tiny foot in the door as he tried to close it on her, grunting softly when the heavy weight of the hand-carved oak hit the side of her arch. He looked down as if he couldn't believe she'd done that, then shot her an angry look.

Figuring he was about a breath away from shoving her back she said, "I'm Ryssa."

He stilled, his gaze growing even colder, if that was possible. She withheld the urge to shiver again. The ice in his human eyes made Marcella seem warm in comparison.

"Ryssa." He repeated the name, but made no move to invite her in or push her away. "Is that supposed to mean something to me?"

For a moment, Ryssa had her doubts. Maybe Marcella had been mistaken. Maybe this wasn't the right place after all, though it would have been hard to mistake this house for any other. Her weight shifted from one foot to the other as she pulled the thin jacket tighter around her in the chill of the night.

"My friend said a woman was asking for me."

Those perfectly cold, clear, green eyes narrowed on her. "Your friend? Who is your friend?"

No way was Ryssa going to tell him about Marcella. Wealthy types like him didn't typically buy into the supernatural. Money, power, prestige – that's what they understood. Not that any of that truly mattered in the grand scheme of things, but it sure as hell wasn't Ryssa's job to enlighten him.

Tired, cranky, and slightly unnerved by the power of his gaze, she opted for the direct approach. "Is someone here dying?"

He winced at that, the only crack in his icy

façade. Behind the frosty exterior, she could sense his pain. It was the only reason she didn't knee him in his manly bits and beat feet out of there. People handled grief in different ways; maybe his was just by being a condescending asshole.

He stared at her like she was some kind of cockroach heading towards the caviar.

"Look," she said, reaching for her patience. "She called, I came. That's how it works. Let me in or release me from the summons."

Avoiding the cold steel of his glare, she looked up at the position of the moon. At most, she had about an hour and a half before she had to turn and go back. Even cutting through the woods it was a long walk and she was beyond tired, having worked nearly a full shift at the *Seven Circles* before coming here.

Still he made no move one way or the other. "Dude, come on. I'm on a schedule here."

His scowl deepened and his fists clenched, but she stood her ground. He might think he was big and bad, but he had no idea what was out there, the ones she dealt with on a regular basis. There were a very limited number of beings who could intimidate her, and they were a whole lot bigger and badder than this GQ jack-off.

Just when she was sure he was going to push her back and slam the door in her face, he stepped back abruptly and opened it instead.

"Follow me. And don't touch anything."

Also by Abbie Zanders

Contemporary Romance

- 📖 Dangerous Secrets (Callaghan Brothers #1)
- 📖 First and Only (Callaghan Brothers #2)
- 📖 House Calls (Callaghan Brothers #3)
- 📖 Seeking Vengeance (Callaghan Brothers #4)
- 📖 Guardian Angel (Callaghan Brothers #5)
- 📖 Beyond Affection (Callaghan Brothers #6)
- 📖 Having Faith (Callaghan Brothers #7)
- 📖 Bottom Line (Callaghan Brothers #8)
- 📖 Forever Mine (Callaghan Brothers #9)
- 📖 Five Minute Man (Covendale Series #1)
- 📖 All Night Woman (Covendale Series #2)
- 📖 The Realist
- 📖 Celestial Desire
- 📖 Celina (Connelly Cousins #1)
- 📖 Johnny (Connelly Cousins #2)
- 📖 Michael (Connelly Cousins #3) – includes bonus novella Jamie (Connelly Cousins #1.5)

Time Travel Romance

- 📖 Maiden in Manhattan
- 📖 Raising Hell in the Highlands

Paranormal

📖 Vampire, Unaware
📖 Black Wolfe's Mate (as Avelyn McCrae)

Historical

📖 A Warrior's Heart (as Avelyn McCrae)

About the Author

Abbie Zanders loves to read and write romance in all forms; she is quite obsessive, really. Her ultimate fantasy is to spend all of her free time doing both, preferably in a secluded mountain cabin overlooking a pristine lake, though a private beach on a lush tropical island works, too. Sharing her work with others of similar mind is a dream come true. She promises her readers two things: no cliffhangers, and there will always be a happy ending. Beyond that, you never know…

Made in the USA
Middletown, DE
06 June 2016